True Crime People & Places

To Anita
Best Wishes
Linda Sage

Linda Sage copywrite © 2024 Linda Sage

All rights reserved.

ISBN: 9798345308363

True Crime People & Places

DEDICATION

With gratitude to everyone who has supported and helped me over the years

To great friendships.

CONTENTS

Introduction	vii
Part 1 – Men Who Kill	13
Part 2 – Women Who Kill	41
Part 3 – Children Who Kill	89
Part 4 – Myth Busting	95
Part 5 – Linda's Insights	101
Part 6 – Serial Killer Articles	129
Part 7 – FAQs for Linda	135
Part 8 – Coercive Control & Stalking	159
Part 9 - True Crime Places	235
Part 10 - Close	249

True Crime People & Places

DISCLAIMER

True crime people & places is a work of non-fiction that explores real-life cases of criminal behaviour, including acts of violence, murder, and other disturbing actions. While every effort has been made to accurately portray these events and the individuals involved.

The views and opinions expressed in this book are those of the author, linda sage, and do not necessarily reflect the views of any individuals, organisations, or institutions mentioned within. Linda sage is a writer with extensive experience in the field of true crime, but her interpretations and analyses are subjective and open to interpretation.

Readers are advised that the content of this book may be unsettling or triggering, as it delves into the darkest aspects of human behaviour.

Discretion is advised, especially for those who may be sensitive to graphic descriptions of violence or explicit language.

Furthermore, true crime people & places is Intended for informational and educational purposes only. It is not intended to glamorise or glorify criminal behaviour, but rather to provide insight into the complex factors that contribute to such actions and to stimulate discussion and understanding. While every effort has been made to ensure the accuracy and reliability of the information presented, the author and publisher cannot guarantee that all details are entirely factual or up-to-date. Readers are encouraged to conduct their own research and consult reliable sources for further information on the cases discussed in this book.

By choosing to read True Crime People & Places, readers acknowledge and accept the inherent risks associated with engaging with true crime literature and agree to approach the subject matter with sensitivity and respect for the victims and their families.

Introduction

Going back to basics has been a long journey for me, a lot of twists, turns, tears and laughter along the way. I, like many have tried various times to pull away, change track, but each time something pulls me back.

As a child I did not imagine a world of savagery and death, my blessed upbringing was due to a wonderfully insightful mother and a very practical, logical father. I can still remember vividly the disappointment of my father when I announced I had signed up for psychology, he had visions of a doctor or a lawyer....... Psychology to him was something you did if you could not do anything else.

My mum on the other hand was wiser than her time, she believed you can do anything you want to if you work at it, this was instilled in me from an early age and I have been extremely lucky that in my lifetime many changes have occurred in the mental health field, many developments and many fabulous research papers, but still we have not concrete answer to what makes a person into a serial killer, there are individuals from all backgrounds, ages and creeds, just as society is.

Sex offences, have been going on from the

beginning of time in all cultures, even in today's society child brides in some cultures is an accepted practice. The most notorious offenders in our history books are those that attack strangers, in reality this is less than two percent, the reason that most sex offenders maintain anonymity is because of their close relationship to the victim, protecting the victim also means protecting the perpetrator.

There is no doubt that the invention of the internet has facilitated interaction and communication between like minded perverted individuals, into underground networks. Crime detection has also developed with this tool, but the battle goes on.

Murder, the classification between murder and manslaughter is the premeditation and in all honesty, I think that every individual at some time or other is capable of manslaughter and many individuals are very fortunate that they have not become a killer. Rage, alcohol, drugs and even many mental health issues on the autistic spectrum span a wide range of strong emotions and behaviours.

There have been some individuals that I have met that I can honestly say "but for the grace of God," had I been in their shoes, would I have done something different? Thankfully, I was not,

but as an individual I fully comprehend and empathise with what they did and why. I am not condoning
any killing, but in the UK we lack the option of a crime of passion, but many judges, solicitors and police officers can understand mitigating circumstances.

Psychopaths, this is probably the widest and possibly the most confusing area for many people, it still amazes me that we in society can have people with psychopathic traits in highly respected positions and forgive their insensitivity and intolerance and a lot of the same characteristics are found in our most heinous and infamous criminals.

There is no doubt that like the autistic spectrum, psychopathy has a spectrum as well, many people have psychopathic traits, but are not violent killers, many of whom you can find in senior management and leadership positions, but all of our notorious killers and serial rapists have some of these traits too. There is still a lot of good investigative research going on showing who crosses that line and why.

In this book I want to share some of my experiences, knowledge and insights into what I have seen throughout my working lifetime. In four decades, it seems incredible how fast that time has gone and how much has changed, but still mental health is a secretive subject, taboo for many and a topic, that unless you or somebody lose to you is affected, society chooses to ignore.

The media without a doubt has a huge responsibility for the interest and intrigue into the criminal world, a world shrouded in mystery and entertainment companies manipulate and distort reality that many then believe to be the truth.

There is no glamour in killing, inflicting pain, coercive control, addictions or being in prison, the reality is that many lives are affected by all of these.

Youth crime without a doubt is increasing, an elderly prison population and the ever increasing number of life tariffs which are often over thirty years of incarceration all give rise to many issues for prisons and their staff.

There is no doubt that crime has changed in my lifetime and there is still a lot to come, but hate and intolerance are fuelling many grassroots crime, before even looking at the more sophisticated element. Without an adequate regime what will our next generations of criminal be like?

In this book we are going to be taking a look at:

True Crime People & Places

Serial Killers, Sex Offenders, Murderers and Psychopaths, in each section there will be facts, insights, my thoughts and experiences. Let's dive into the murky world of serious crime.

True Crime People & Places

True Crime People & Places

Part 1
Men Who Kill

Reg Christie

Gave false evidence to convict Timothy Evan of his own murderous crimes.

John Reginald Halliday Christie (8 April 1899 – 15 July 1953), better known to his family and friends as Reg Christie. He is a convicted serial killer and alleged necrophile. He was active in the 1940s and 1950s, whilst living in his ground floor flat at 10 Rillington Place, Notting Hill, London.

His crimes were discovered after he moved out in March 1953. Three bodies of his victims were found in a boarded up alcove in the kitchen, which he had wallpapered over. Remains of two more victims' bodies were dug up in the garden and his wife was found under the floorboards of the front room of the flat. All of his victims had been strangled. He was arrested, charged and convicted of his wife's murder and sentenced to hang, he was subsequently executed in HMP Pentonville, London on the 15th Jury, 1953.

However, if this legacy was not enough; Timothy Evans with his wife Beryl and daughter Geraldine has been neighbours in a 3rd floor flat in the same building as Reg between 1948 and 1949, Beryl and Geraldine were both murdered, Timothy was arrested and convicted, but protested his innocence throughout, he even accused Reg Christie and talked to the police about him. Reg Christie was a major prosecution witness in his trial. Timothy was executed at Pentonville prison on the 9th March, 1950.

Three years later, when Reg's crimes all came to light, doubt was shed on the conviction and execution of Timothy Evans. Reg Christie did admit to the killing of Beryl, but denied killing the daughter, it was widely accepted that he did indeed kill 8 people including Geraldine.

Because of the flawed way the Timothy Evans investigation was conducted being blinkered into only considering the husband, Reg Christie went on to kill four more victims before his detection.

In 2004, 54 years after his death, Timothy Evans had his conviction quashed by the High Court, accepting that Timothy did not kill his wife or child.

Stephen Shaun Griffiths, the Crossbow Cannibal

Convicted of the three Bradford murders but could be responsible for more.

Stephen Shaun Griffiths was born 24 December 1969 in Dewsbury, West Riding of Yorkshire, one of several serial killers originating from this part of England. He was convicted various time from a young age for offences with knives and had served previous sentences for violent crimes.

Three sex worker women disappeared from Bradford between 2009 and 2010, Susan Rushworth (43), was first on the 22nd June, 2009, next Shelley Armitage (31) on the 26th April, 2010 and Suzanne Blmires (36) on the 21st May also in 2010.

The river Aire, in Shipley gave up some of Suzanne's remains on the 25th May, other human tissue reclaimed from the river was identified to be from Shelley, however no remains have ever been found for Susan.

Stephen then 40 was arrested on the 24th May, later charged, when he was sworn in he stated his name was Crossbow Killer. Via a video link from Wakefield prison his case was heard in Crown

Court on the 16th November, 2010 and convicted of killing all three women, on the 21st December, after he pleaded guilty for this he received a Full Life Tariff, which means he will never be released from prison.

On his being interviewed in 2010 Stephen claimed to police that there were more victims, he said he had killed 6 women, however after his conviction for the three women, he refused to speak to police officers again, so no further ties to sex worker crimes have been made.

Stephen, has attempted suicide in a number of occasions whilst in prison and in 2011 had a 2 month hunger strike, but now well into his fifties he is still serving his sentence.

Mark Robinson

10 years served for murder, 7 months of freedom, then he killed again

Mark Robinson at 17 years old had joined the RAF, on his home leave during the Spring Bank Holiday, he went to a neighbours house Mrs Patricia Wagner, pretending to be drunk, with the intention of having sex with her.

He talked his way into her home and when she said she would tell his mother, Mark got angry, he punched her in the face, she tried to defend herself, so he threw her on the floor and kicked her, then he strangled her with the cord of a table lamp and left her body where it lay on the floor of her living room, for her 8 year old son to find.

He was arrested just hours later and convicted in 1979 to life imprisonment, he served ten years and was released in March 1989.

He met Sharon Morley in Wakefield and the two ended up moving to Billingham. This was a tempestuous, toxic relationship with many arguments. Sharon wanted to move back to Wakefield, Mark did not, Mark found a picture of Sharon's former boyfriend, the 19th September 1989 just 7 months later he beat her and stabbed the 25 year old Sharon to death.

Newcastle Crown Court told him that this life sentence would mean a life order.

In 2011, 6ft 2 in, 20 stone Mark added another three years to his sentence when 5 prison officers were assaulted in Wakefield prison, putting them in hospital, after his bread ration was cut.

Raoul Moat

In the summer of 2010, the Northumbria Police found themselves in the midst of a harrowing manhunt that gripped the nation. The target: Raoul Moat, a 37-year-old ex-prisoner who had unleashed a wave of violence, leaving one person dead, two wounded, and an entire region on edge.

The Shooting Spree: The tragic saga began with a two-day shooting spree in July 2010.

Moat's victims included his ex-girlfriend Samantha Stobbart, her new partner Chris Brown, and police officer David Rathband. Armed with a sawn-off shotgun, Moat's actions sent shockwaves through Tyne and Wear, leaving a trail of devastation that would scar the community for years to come.

Victims and Fallout: Samantha Stobbart, hospitalized, but fortunate to survive, bore witness to the brutality of Moat's actions. Tragically, Chris Brown lost his life, and police officer David Rathband faced not only near-fatal injuries, but also a life-changing consequence, permanent blindness. Rathband valiantly fought through the darkness, but haunted by the events, succumbed to suicide on February 29, 2012.

The Manhunt Unfolds: Following the shooting spree, Raoul Moat went on the run, eluding the police for nearly a week. The manhunt, spanning Tyne and Wear and Northumberland was a monumental police operation. The community anxiously awaited news, and the authorities faced the daunting task of capturing a man driven to the brink.

Rothbury Standoff: The manhunt reached its climax near the town of Rothbury, Northumberland. In a tense six-hour standoff, armed police officers, under the command of the Northumbria Police, confronted Moat. Ultimately, Moat's desperate escape came to a tragic end when he took his own life, a chilling conclusion to a week of terror.

Legacy of Tragedy: The Raoul Moat case left an indelible mark on the affected families and the wider community. It also sparked debates about the challenges of dealing with individuals struggling with mental health issues and the potential dangers of releasing ex-prisoners back into society.

Conclusion: The 2010 Northumbria Police manhunt stands as a sombre reminder of the destructive power of unchecked violence and the profound impact it can have on individuals and communities. As we reflect on this tragic chapter, it underscores the ongoing importance of addressing mental health challenges and fostering a society that seeks to prevent, rather than respond to, such heart breaking incidents.

Babes in the Wood

In the tranquil woodlands near Moulsecoomb, Brighton, the 9 October 1986, witnessed a tragedy that would leave an indelible mark on criminal history. The brutal murder of two young cousins, Karen Hadaway and Nicola Fellows, raised not only questions about the motives behind such heinous acts but also cast a long shadow of uncertainty over the years. The resolution of the case, with the conviction of Russell Bishop in 2018, unveils a chilling tale that spans over three decades.

The Perplexing Crime: The Babes in the Wood case is as perplexing as it is tragic. Two innocent lives cut short in the serene backdrop of a woodland, leaving a community in shock and investigators grappling with the intricacies of the crime. The details of the case prompt us to delve into the motives and psychology behind such acts of violence against the most vulnerable members of society.

Russell Bishop: A Decades-Long Pursuit of Justice: The turning point in this chilling narrative came on December 10, 2018, when Russell Bishop was convicted and sentenced to two life terms with a minimum of 36 years in prison. This verdict marked the culmination of a tireless pursuit of justice that spanned more than three decades. The case, initially marred by challenges and setbacks, eventually saw a breakthrough that would bring closure to the victims' families and the community at large.

DNA: The Silent Witness: A crucial element in the resolution of the case was the role played by DNA evidence. It took 32 years for advancements in forensic technology to provide the necessary breakthrough. The silent witness finally spoke, linking Russell Bishop to the crime scene and bringing justice to the long-suffering families. This technological leap underscores the importance of continued advancements in forensic science in solving cold cases.

Motives and Psychology: The conviction of Russell Bishop prompts a revisiting of the motives and psychology behind the crime. What drove an individual to commit such a heinous act against innocent children, and how did the passage of time influence the investigation?

These questions invite us to explore the dark corners of criminal behaviour and the impact of unresolved cases on the collective psyche of a community.

Conclusion: The resolution of the Babes in the Wood case serves as a testament to the resilience of those seeking justice and the power of advancements in forensic science. As we reflect on this decades-long journey, we are reminded of the importance of perseverance in the face of adversity and the role technology plays in unravelling the mysteries of the past. The Babes in the Wood case, once shrouded in uncertainty, now stands as a beacon of hope for those still awaiting answers.

The Suffolk Strangler - Steve Wright

In the annals of criminal psychology and true crime, the name Steve Wright, known as the Suffolk Strangler, stands out as a grim reminder of the darkness that can lurk within seemingly ordinary individuals. This article delves into the life and crimes of Steve Wright, shedding light on his twisted path of violence and the intricate web of investigations that eventually led to his capture.

Early Life: Born on July 24, 1958, in Norfolk, England, Steve Wright had an unremarkable childhood. He grew up in a modest family and didn't exhibit any early signs of the horrifying criminal activities he would later engage in. Wright's quiet upbringing makes his descent into infamy all the more perplexing to psychologists.

The Murders: Steve Wright's heinous crimes took place in Ipswich, Suffolk, over a short and terrifying timespan. Between October and December 2006, he brutally abducted and murdered five women before transporting them to their isolated deposition sites, all of whom were involved in sex work. His victims were Tania Nicol, Gemma Adams, Anneli Alderton, Annette Nicholls, and Paula Clennell. The chilling similarity in their deaths sent shockwaves through the community.

Investigation and Capture: The Suffolk Strangler case sparked one of the most extensive and challenging investigations in British criminal history. Law enforcement agencies collaborated to track down the killer. Advanced forensic techniques, including DNA analysis and surveillance footage, played crucial roles in narrowing down their search. Finally, on December 19, 2006, Steve Wright was arrested, when tiny flecks of blood were found on the back seats of Wright's car that partially matched the DNA profile of murder victim Paula Clennell, then his connection to the murders became apparent.

Psychological Evaluation: During his trial, Wright stated he had gone to professional prostitutes on many occasions throughout his life, including three of the murder victims. Wright is still being investigated in connection with other unsolved murders and disappearances.

Experts have highlighted how it is unlikely for any serial killer to start killing with such precision at such a late stage (Wright was 48 years old when the 2006 murders were committed), and that serial killers almost always start killing before their mid 30s. This indicates that Wright likely killed before in his life. It's a stark reminder that the human mind can harbour unimaginable darkness.

Conclusion: Steve Wright's reign of terror as the Suffolk Strangler serves as a stark reminder of the complexities that lie within the realm of criminal psychology. His case raises numerous questions about what drives an individual to commit such gruesome acts. Understanding the criminal mindset is essential for society as a whole, as it helps us prevent and respond to such tragedies.

21 February 2008, at Ipswich Crown Court, Wright was sentenced to life imprisonment with the recommendation that he should never be released.

The Yorkshire Ripper - Peter Sutcliffe

Peter Sutcliffe, infamously known as the "Yorkshire Ripper," stands as one of the most notorious serial killers in the history of criminal psychology. His reign of terror in the 1970s and 1980 left a trail of fear and bloodshed across West Yorkshire and beyond. What made Peter Sutcliffe so dangerous? In this article, we will delve into the factors that contributed to his terrifying notoriety.

Cunning Manipulation

One of the key aspects that made Peter Sutcliffe exceptionally dangerous was his ability to manipulate those around him, particularly in West Yorkshire. He appeared to be an ordinary man, leading a seemingly mundane life as a truck driver in Bradford. This facade allowed him to evade suspicion and continue his gruesome murders for an extended period.

Victim Selection
Sutcliffe's meticulous selection of victims, including those in Leeds and Bradford, played a crucial role in his danger. He primarily targeted sex workers, knowing that they were less likely to be reported missing quickly. This strategic choice allowed him to remain elusive to law enforcement throughout West Yorkshire.

Prolific Murder Spree
Sutcliffe's sheer number of victims in and around West Yorkshire is a testament to his level of danger. Over a five-year period, he claimed the lives of at least 13 women and attempted to murder several more. His ability to strike repeatedly without being apprehended intensified the fear in the community, including Leeds and Bradford.

Eluding Capture
Sutcliffe's ability to evade capture for such an extended period of time baffled law enforcement not only in West Yorkshire but also nationwide. Despite being interviewed multiple times during the investigation, he managed to deflect suspicion and continue his killing spree.

Psychopathic Traits
Psychopathy is characterised by traits such as superficial charm, lack of empathy, and a propensity for violence. Sutcliffe displayed many of these traits, making it difficult for people to recognise the darkness that lurked within him.

Taunting Letters & Tapes

The letters and tapes sent to the authorities, taunting the police and media added an extra layer of danger to his profile, further instilling fear in both local and national communities. There is always the question did the heinous sidetracking of John Samuel Humble cost some victims their lives and would Sutcliffe have been caught earlier?

Psychological Profiling

Sutcliffe's case played a pivotal role in the development of criminal profiling, not only in modus operandi and victim selection were carefully analysed by experts, contributing to the understanding of serial killers and their patterns.

Community Panic
The fear generated by Peter Sutcliffe reached a fever pitch in West Yorkshire, including Leeds and Bradford. Women were terrified to venture out alone, and the public was on high alert. This widespread panic added to the danger he posed to the community.

Conclusion

In the annals of criminal psychology, Peter Sutcliffe's name will forever be associated with danger and terror in West Yorkshire, encompassing areas such as Leeds, Bradford, and the wider region. His cunning manipulation, victim selection, and psychopathic traits made him a truly menacing figure.

Sutcliffe's ability to elude capture, coupled with the fear he instilled in the community, marks him as one of the most dangerous serial killers in history. His case continues to serve as a chilling reminder of the depths of human depravity in West Yorkshire and beyond.

Delayed Justice for Brian Lunn Field

In the tranquil suburb of Surrey, the year was 1968 when tragedy struck the Tutill family.

Fourteen-year-old Roy Tutill, a schoolboy full of dreams and innocence, met a horrific fate that would haunt the community for decades. His murder remained a chilling unsolved mystery until the astonishing revelation in 2001 when DNA evidence led to the apprehension of the long-elusive killer, Brian Lunn Field. This is the story of Roy Tutill's murder, a 33-year-old cold case that finally found justice through the marvels of modern forensic science.

The Tragic Day: April 23, 1968

On that fateful day in 1968, young Roy Tutill was walking home from school, completely unaware of the harrowing ordeal that awaited him. His life was cut short in a heinous act that sent shockwaves through the peaceful community of Surrey. The circumstances surrounding his rape and murder were nothing short of a nightmare for his family and the entire town. The loss of a beloved child left a scar that would never truly heal.

Decades of Mystery

As the years passed, Roy Tutill's murder became a cold case, shrouded in darkness. Despite the efforts of law enforcement, the case remained unsolved, leaving a cloud of uncertainty hanging over the Tutill family and the community at large. The torment of not knowing who had taken their son's life weighed heavily on his family.

The Turning Point: DNA Evidence

The breakthrough that would eventually lead to justice came in 2001, 33 long years after Roy Tutill's murder. DNA evidence, a powerful tool in modern forensic science, played a pivotal role. It was this evidence that finally led investigators to Brian Lunn Field, a man who had eluded justice for decades. Field's confession to the crime sent shockwaves through the community once again, as the truth behind one of Surrey's most notorious cold cases was finally exposed.

Impact on Cold Case Investigations

The resolution of Roy Tutill's case has had far reaching implications. It showcased the immense potential of DNA evidence in cracking even the oldest and most seemingly unsolvable cold cases. The Tutill case served as a beacon of hope for law enforcement agencies working on similar cases across the globe. It emphasized the importance of perseverance and the continuous advancements in forensic technology.

A Changing Landscape

The breakthrough in the Roy Tutill case was not an isolated incident. It marked a turning point in how cold cases are viewed and investigated.

Subsequent cases, such as the conviction of David Burgess for the 1966 murder of Yolande Waddington in 2012, further demonstrated the transformative power of DNA evidence. These cases have brought closure to grieving families and rekindled faith in the criminal justice system.

Conclusion

The murder of Roy Tutill in 1968, followed by 33 years of mystery and uncertainty, serves as a poignant reminder of the importance of never giving up on justice. Through the remarkable capabilities of DNA evidence, the cold case was finally solved, and Brian Lunn Field was brought to justice, sentenced to a life imprisonment. Roy Tutill's memory lives on, not just as a victim, but as a symbol of resilience, determination, and the enduring quest for truth and justice in even the most challenging cases.

The Kray Twins: Notorious Icons of the East End

In the annals of criminal history, few names resonate as powerfully as that of the Kray Twins, Ronnie and Reggie. These identical twins, born in London's East End, rose to infamy as some of the most notorious gangsters of their time. In this article, we'll delve into the lives of the Kray Twins and explore their deep-rooted connection to the gritty streets of the East End.

Early Life: Ronnie and Reggie Kray were born on October 24, 1933, in Hoxton, a district in London's East End. They were raised in a working-class family, and their upbringing was far from glamorous. Growing up amidst the poverty and post-war turmoil of the East End, they developed a fierce loyalty to each other that would define their criminal empire.

The Rise to Power: The Kray Twins initially dabbled in amateur boxing and legitimate business ventures, such as nightclubs. However, their ambitions soon took a darker turn. In the 1950s and 1960s, they began consolidating their power in the criminal underworld, establishing protection rackets, and becoming involved in organised crime activities.

East End Notoriety: The East End of London, with its tight-knit communities and working-class neighbourhoods, provided the perfect backdrop for the Kray Twins' criminal activities. The brothers exploited their local connections and instilled fear in the hearts of residents and business owners alike. The area became a hotbed of their criminal enterprises, from extortion to brutal acts of violence.

The Celebrity Connection: One unique aspect of the Kray Twins' notoriety was their fascination with fame. They rubbed shoulders with celebrities, including actors and musicians, which only added to their mystique. Their East End nightclub the Double R Club, and the infamous The Blind Beggar pub, became popular hangouts for both underworld figures and the glitterati of London's entertainment scene.

Legal Troubles: As their criminal empire expanded, so did the attention from law enforcement. The Kray Twins faced numerous arrests, but their reign of terror continued for years. Eventually, they were convicted of murder and sentenced to life imprisonment in 1969.

Legacy: The Kray Twins' legacy endures in both criminal history and pop culture. Their story has been immortalised in books, films, and documentaries. While some glamorise their criminal exploits, others see them as symbols of the darker side of the East End's history.

In Prison: March 1969, when they were sentenced for the murders of rival gangsters George Cornell and Jack McVitie. Ronnie and Reggie were both sentenced at London's Old Bailey court, receiving sentences of life imprisonment with 30 years of non-parole. They were, at the time, the longest sentences ever passed at the Old Bailey.

The Krays continued to run a protection racket from prison. Their bodyguard business, Krayleigh Enterprises, supplied Frank Sinatra with 18 bodyguards in 1985.

In Death: Ronnie Kray died in Broadmoor high-security psychiatric hospital in 1995, from a heart attack.

Reggie passed away from cancer in 2000. He had been released from prison on compassionate grounds.

They are buried in Chingford Mount Cemetery, East London.

Conclusion: The Kray Twins, Ronnie and Reggie, left an indelible mark on the East End of London. Their story serves as a cautionary tale of how power, ambition, and a strong sense of brotherhood can lead down a destructive path.

While the East End has evolved since their era, the legend of the Kray Twins remains deeply embedded in the history of this iconic London neighbourhood.

A Profound Examination of Peter Tobin's Disturbing Odyssey

A gripping exploration into the life and crimes of Peter Tobin, in our True Crime People and Places spotlight. A haunting figure whose narrative is etched into the chilling tapestry of criminal history. Let's embark on an immersive journey to unravel the intricacies of Tobin's story, casting a piercing light into the shadowy recesses of the human psyche.

The Early Years: Our odyssey commences in the heart of Johnstone, Renfrewshire, in 1946, where the threads of Peter Tobin's early life weave a narrative of hardship and adversity. Set against a canvas of challenges, Tobin's formative years unfold with complexities that lay the groundwork for the disconcerting path he would ultimately traverse.

Criminal Beginnings: Tobin's initial foray into the realm of criminality spans a spectrum from petty theft to disturbing instances of sexual assault. These early chapters offer a tantalising glimpse into the tumultuous journey that would eventually lead him down a far more sinister and ominous road.

Notorious Crimes: The zenith of Tobin's criminal saga unveils a sequence of bone-chilling murders and rapes, with the names Vicky Hamilton, Dinah McNicol, and Angelika Kluk echoing through the corridors of infamy. These cases, each more harrowing than the last, not only shocked the nation but prompted a collective introspection into the malevolent workings of a criminal mind.

Psychological Analysis: As we assume the role of armchair investigators, the imperative lies in scrutinising the psychological intricacies that underpin Tobin's nefarious actions. A nuanced exploration reveals a kaleidoscope of factors, from a turbulent upbringing to a profoundly skewed moral compass, all converging to mold a perpetrator capable of orchestrating such grievous acts.

Impact on Society: Beyond the individual horror of Tobin's crimes, our gaze widens to encompass the broader societal ripples. The fear instilled by his actions serves as a stark reminder of the ongoing need for rigorous research, heightened awareness, and proactive preventative measures within the realm of criminal psychology.

Conclusion: As we draw the curtain on this mesmerising journey into the enigma of Peter Tobin, let us collectively reflect on the profound lessons embedded in his dark tale. Through the unravelling of the layers of the human psyche, we empower ourselves to comprehend the intricate factors that can propel an individual down a perilous and treacherous path.

A Pattern of Violence: Robert Napper's Criminal Offences

Napper's offenses escalated in a pattern that we frequently observe in violent criminals: from voyeurism and stalking to sexual assault, and ultimately, murder. His criminal record includes a series of violent attacks and sexual assaults, often targeting women in parks or secluded areas. Known as the "Green Chain Rapist," he was suspected of committing at least 70 sexual assaults in London during the late 1980s and early 1990s, though he was only formally charged with a fraction of these offences.

One of the most notorious cases linked to Napper is the 1992 murder of Rachel Nickell on Wimbledon Common, a crime for which another man, Colin Stagg, was initially wrongfully accused. Napper's involvement in the case was overlooked for years, as investigators focused on Stagg, whose evidence was later quashed. This case highlights the devastating consequences of investigative bias and illustrates how easily a dangerous offender can remain active when law enforcement misjudges evidence.

In 1993, Napper committed another horrific act, the murder of Samantha Bisset and her four-year-old daughter, Jazmine, in their London home. The level of violence was shockingly brutal, and this crime further underscored Napper's profound capacity for sadism. His actions left a lasting mark on British criminal history, raising questions about how offenders like Napper can go undetected despite a history of violence.

The Psychological Profile of Robert Napper
Robert Napper's crimes offer a disturbing window into the mind of a violent, psychotic offender. Diagnosed with paranoid schizophrenia and Asperger's syndrome, Napper exhibited profound delusions and an obsession with sexual violence. These conditions, paired with the effects of his abusive and neglected childhood, may have contributed to his inability to empathize or control his violent urges.

From a psychological standpoint, Napper's profile fits within what experts might categorise as a highly disorganised offender with psychotic tendencies. Unlike offenders who carefully plan and organise their attacks, disorganised offenders often act on impulse, leaving behind chaotic crime scenes that reflect their inner turmoil. Napper's crimes were frequently characterised by excessive violence and post-mortem mutilation, signaling the expression of deeply rooted rage and unresolved psychological distress.

Failures in the System: Lessons from Napper's Case

The case of Robert Napper highlights several flaws within the criminal justice system, particularly regarding the handling of mentally ill offenders. Napper had been in contact with mental health professionals and law enforcement multiple times before his most heinous acts. Reports suggest that he was assessed by psychiatrists and placed on medication, but consistent, coordinated intervention appears to have been lacking.

Additionally, investigative tunnel vision, as seen in the Rachel Nickell case, demonstrates the risks of prematurely focusing on a suspect without thoroughly considering alternative leads. Napper's behaviour and violent tendencies were known, yet law enforcement was diverted by the Stagg investigation. In hindsight, had Napper been apprehended earlier, the lives of Samantha and Jazmine Bisset, and possibly other victims, might have been spared.

Reflection: The Importance of Understanding and Intervention

The case of Robert Napper emphasizes the importance of early intervention in cases of severe mental illness. Psychotic disorders, such as paranoid schizophrenia, can significantly impair judgment and impulse control, sometimes leading to violent behaviour if left untreated. The lesson here is not to stigmatise mental illness, but rather to understand the critical need for accessible, effective treatment and monitoring, particularly for those with violent tendencies or criminal histories.

Forensic psychology and criminal profiling have advanced considerably since Napper's time, and lessons from his case have informed better protocols for dealing with suspects who exhibit similar psychological markers. Napper's case underscores the importance of understanding the complexities of the criminal mind, especially in cases where mental health issues intersect with violent crime.

Closing Thoughts

The story of Robert Napper is as tragic as it is terrifying. His case is a stark reminder of the importance of early intervention, the dangers of investigative biases, and the need for a better understanding of mental illness in the context of criminal behaviour. In exploring the minds of individuals like Napper, we gain insights into the complex and disturbing factors that can culminate in violent crime, as well as the systemic changes needed to prevent future tragedies.

True Crime People & Places

Part 2:
Women Who Kill

Women kill less than men.

Although, many readers and writers of crime novels are female, fewer fictional murderers are and still fewer real life killers are women.

Women are reflected most often as the victims, increasingly in the sleuths, or leading detectives, rarely as perpetrators. While women do kill within the pages of novels, these are often one time acts with a single victim, a crime of passion, an act of protection or self-defense, rarer is the woman who makes murder her life's purpose.

However, as demonstrated by Shay Groves who was imprisoned for life, on the 22nd February, 2023, for the horrific slaying of her boyfriend, with 17 stab wounds to his chest and cutting his throat, all because she thought he was texting another girl.

Her rogues gallery consisted of framed pictures of the most notorious serial killers, she was obsessed with knowing about them, their crimes and their motivations. She also had a collection of true crime books and a variety of knives, Viking axes and a Celtic dagger.

True life crime often reflects novels and vice versa, with horrific outcomes. Yet another family must live with fatal outcome of a true crime obsession.

It is still hard for society to accept the concept of a woman killing, and even less that children kill, but although the numbers are much lower, they do exist. That could be the reason why the media and entertainment make their names even more notorious. Synonymous with British female murdering notoriety are Myra Hindley, Rose West, Beverley Allitt, and Joanna Dennehy over the years they have come to represent the evilest of women, but there are many more female killers in our prisons.

Myra was the only one here that did not kill alone and had she not met Ian Brady, would her life have been different, that is a huge debate that continues. Rose, Beverley and Joanna all killed alone and killed many times over. That is what is most intriguing for many people.

Murder is very different to serial murder and there are still a significant number of female killers, over 50% of female killers are over 35 years old, whereas the highest age groups of male perpetrators are younger.

Trying to understand these women, unravel their reasons for killing are often very complex and toxic relationships have shadowed their lives.

Children who kill often bring communities to a

standstill, from our youngest serial killer James Fairweather at just fifteen picking his victims at random, to Kim Edwards and Lucas Markham who were just 14-years-old when they killed Kim's mum and 13-year old sister, or Sharon Louise Carr, who is Britain's youngest female murderer, aged only 12, Of course this section cannot forget the two young boys who stunned a nation with their brutal abduction, torture and murder of two year old James Bulger, namely, Robert Thompson and Jon Venables, both just 10 years old at the time.

How the media portrays women murderers
Do they portray them in a positive or negative light? Do they portray them realistically?

Without a doubt the power of the media has been seen with the sensationalism shown to female killers, they overexpose them and often portray them harshly. They are certainly in the minority compared to males, so when a woman does kill it is certainly headlining news.

Society is fascinated by the fact that women, who are often seen as innocent, fragile, and dependable, can commit such heinous acts. Most of the murders committed by women are due to greed, jealousy, self-defense, revenge, or psychopathology.

Prior to World War 1 some female killers used poison and went undetected for years, mainly because the governing male society did not think they were capable or intelligent enough to kill.

Throughout history, female murderers have been considered a rare and unique breed of criminal. When the crimes are especially heinous and against perceived female norms, the court system, media, and public come down exceedingly hard on these unnatural and doubly deviant criminals.

Myra Hindley dubbed the Most Evil Woman in Britain, because she showed no remorse, she did not shed a tear in court. There was and still is many decades after she was convicted a media and societal interest in her and her life.

Rafter and Stanko in their 1982 publication identified six images of women that influence how they are perceived in both society and the criminal justice system:

The "pawn of biology" in which women are viewed as "gripped by biological forces beyond [their] control.

"Impulsive and non-analytical" in which women seemingly act intuitively and illogically;

"Passive and weak" in which women are seen as easy prey for victimisation or compliant accomplices.

" Impressionable and in need of protection" in which

women are viewed as #gullible and easily led astray.

"Active woman as masculine" in which women who break stereotypical passive role as deviant are likely to be criminal and also likely to be viewed as lesbian.

"Purely evil" suggests that it is worse for women to be criminal than for men because women are breaking out both law abiding boundaries and stereotypical gender role boundaries.

Serial killers are also a different breed of criminal, since World War 2 there have only been 4 female serial killers caught in the UK, Myra Hindley, Rose West and Joanna Dennehy and Lucy Letby this is why they are so intensely scrutinised by the media, society and the entertainment world.

Without a doubt their crimes are heinous, but behind bars, they are all just women with strengths and weaknesses, tempers, tears and traumas.

Mary Ann Cotton

Maybe not a name you know, but she was killing her husbands, her children and several others with poisons before Jack the Ripper, officially noted as the first female serial killer.

Mary Ann born in 1832 in Durham, for nearly a

decade poisoned four of her husbands, two lodgers and fifteen children, and she was getting ready to marry in 1872 husband number five when she got caught for killing seven-year-old Charles, her stepson.

Mary Ann had been claiming insurance money and moving on with her life, when London police became suspicious and investigated her twenty family losses.

Mary Ann had worked as a nurse, so understood the use of arsenic, which was prevalent in the mid Victorian era, and virtually undetectable until James Marsh devised a test to detect it. However, arsenic poisoning was common at the time as its presence was in many everyday items such as children's toys, wallpaper and even in baby carriages.

The effects of the arsenic in Mary Ann's tea, which was her preferred method, were very similar to gastric fever, which had been the diagnosis in the previous deaths of all her victims.

In 1873 her trail began, and she gave birth to her last child in prison, Mary Ann protested her innocence, but the jury only took one hour of deliberation to find her guilty. On the 24th March, 1873 Mary Ann Cotton went to the gallows for her crimes. Britain's first reported female serial killer was written into the history books.

Amelia Elizabeth Dyer - Dubbed the "Ogress of Reading", is the most prolific serial killer in British history with over 400 deaths of babies over a thirty-year span in Victorian England.

Amelia from Bristol, trained as a nurse and was widowed in 1869, Dyer turned to baby farming, the practice of adopting unwanted infants in exchange for money, to support herself.

Illegitimacy in the Victorian society was hugely stigmatised, so Baby Farmers were in demand. Amelia did start off with good intentions and cared for children as well as her own. A number of them died, whether intentionally or not (at this time), lead to a conviction of neglect and six months hard labour.

After her release from prison, she did start Baby Farming again and this time, aimed to kill babies, she usually strangled them, tied some cord around their necks and watch them die.

Mentally unstable for a lot of her adult life, she had several stints in asylums, although these were thought to be at times when she needed to get away as her crimes were catching up with her, however, she survived one major suicide attempt.

She "adopted" babies from single mothers and got paid anything from £5 to £80 depending on the wealth of the family.

Because of this case adoption laws in Britain were tightened up and the newly formed NSPCC, (National Society for the Prevention of Cruelty to Children) was given a lot of attention.

A bargeman on the Thames found a carpet bag with two bodies a small baby Helena Fry and a boy of about fourteen months, both had been strangled, wrapped up and thrown away.

Her capture was not quick, great detective work by DC Anderson and Sgt James, they put Amelia under surveillance, but soon learnt if she felt threatened, she would just move on to another place. They could not risk this, so they set up a decoy to engage her to talk about her services.

On the 3rd April, 1869, the police raided her home and found a huge amount of evidence demonstrating that she had taken receipt of at least 20 children in the previous few months. Six more body of babies were also discovered.

On May 22nd Amelia appeared in the Old Bailey and pleaded guilty to murder, it took a jury only four and a half minutes to find her guilty. In her three weeks in confinement, she wrote over 5 exercise books full about her life, she handed these to a priest on the evening before her execution. Amelia Dyer was executed in Newgate prison on Wednesday, 10th June, 1869.

As Amelia was around at the same time of Jack the

Ripper, it was speculated that she may be involved here too.

Jack or maybe Jill the Ripper?

Mary Pearcey, a convicted English murderer, who has been cited on numerous occasions as a possible candidate for Jack the Ripper.

Mary was active at the same time and her violent tendencies add weight to the suspicion.

Mary Elenor Wheeler, was born in 1866, she took the surname Pearcey from a carpenter John Charles Pearcery who she lived with, but never married. John is reported to have left her due to her infidelities.

She later made a home, in Kentish Town, London, but again did not marry a furniture remover, Frank Hogg, he is reported to have a string of lovers as well. Phoebe Styles was one such affair, but when Phoebe became pregnant Mary pushed Frank to married her. Styles gave birth to a daughter who also took her mother's name Phoebe. This unorthodox family lasted for about 18 months.

October the 24th 1890, Mary invited Phoebe and her daughter round for tea at 4pm. This invitation was to be their last, during the investigation police were told by neighbours that they had heard shouting and screaming.

Later that evening, a woman's body was found on Hampstead Heath with her skull crushed and her head almost severed from her body. A blood soaked black pram was also found in Finchley, the body of a suffocated girl had been left in the pram.
On investigation several sightings of Mary were seen pushing a back pram around the streets of North London after dark. As soon as detectives went to Mary's home they found, blood spatters on the ceiling, walls, skirting and floors as well as on Mary's skirt and apron. There were also clumps of hair, and blood on the fire poker and carving knife.

Mary proclaimed her innocence right through her trial, but was convicted and hung on the 23rd December, 1890

It did not end there, this case caused such notoriety in the press, through the acute violence of a female murderer that Madam Tussaud's produced a wax figure of Mary Pearcey for their Chamber of Horror exhibition, Tussauds also purchased the black pram and the contents of Mary's kitchen for their exhibit, when it opened it drew 30,000 people to see it.

Sir Arthur Conan Doyal as well as other notable writers and journalist at the time linked the possibility of Mary Pearcey to the Ripper murders, with the possibility that a woman could have easy access to these slain women as a nurse or midwife.

More credence was given to the theory of Jill the Ripper in May 2006, when DNA testing of some stamps on letters allegedly sent by Jack the Ripper to London newspapers, genuinely appeared to be female saliva. A whirlwind of global speculation and discussion followed about the involvement of Mary Pearcey in the Ripper murders.

Myra Hindley:

Myra Hindley's Early Life

Myra Hindley has the legacy of being 'the most hated woman in Britain' for her role in the gruesome Moors Murders. Between July 1963 and October 1965.

Long before that Myra was born on 23rd July, 1942, in Crumpsall, a suburb in Manchester. She was the eldest child of Bob Hindley and his wife, Hettie. Bob served in a parachute regiment during World War II so was absent for the majority of the first three years of Myra's life.

Bob returned home to work as a machinist in a factory, they lived in a typical two up-two down terrace house. Being military Bob could be a hard task master and like so many others enjoyed a drink, and was unable to show or share his feelings, which was very typical of society at that time. At the age of four Myra's sister Maureen was born and Myra was sent to live with her grandmother, initially to give them some space with the new baby, but Myra never returned home.

Myra grew up with her grandmother in a working class Manchester suburb. Much has been said over the years about Myra coming from a broken home, being unloved, but she seemed happy to have been in the company of her grandmother, who was more lenient than her father. Plus, her grand- mother's house was very close to her family home, from the windows of her grandmother's house they could see into her parent's home. She was most certainly loved, even if their family arrangements were not all that conventional.

Religion in this household was mixed, Bob was Roman Catholic and Hettie was Church of England, they agreed that if the girls were baptised into the Catholic religion, they would not have to attend Catholic schools. Myra in her primary years did not do so well and failed the 11 plus exam, though at Ryder Brow secondary modern school she was seen as intelligent and very able, but her attendance was poor, because her grandmother did not always insist on her being at school.

Myra was taught by her dad to be tough and stand up for yourself, she did not develop very early and was known for her boyish figure, and a deep voice, she was on the receiving end of a lot of bullying and name calling during her early adolescence.

However, she was respected in her local community and deemed a responsible babysitter by her neighbours, in her teenage years she took many younger children and teens under her protective wing.

In fact, a possible turning point in Myra's life was when at the age of 15, Michael Higgins a boy of 13 she had befriended drowned. Myra really took this to heart as she was a very strong swimmer and always felt he would not have died if she had been there. This event caused her to leave school and take up Roman Catholicism. For three years Myra was very church oriented incredibly modest and deeply believed in God.

At 18 Myra started working as a secretary at Millwards Merchandising, in Manchester and on her first day meet 23 year old Ian Brady in January, 1961. Brady was working as a stock clerk; he had already been to prison. Myra always recollects that meeting as the start of a new life and a new person. His dark hair, deep blue eyes and fresh complexion almost had her fixated on him, but his nails were manicured and she had never seen a man with such clean and cared for nails. He was a snappy dresser, aloof and rode a motorbike, this was intoxicating for the prim and proper Myra.

Myra says she was just totally infatuated with him, he was likewise infatuated with the Nazis and the Aryan propaganda, and obsessed with Adolf Hitler,

Ian was very intelligent and well read, his deep and heated discussions, just fuelled Myra's interest.

There was not much interest in Myra by Ian Brady, according to her recollections he did not even speak to her until the 27th July, but she wanted to get noticed by him. She started to read the books he spoke about, Marquis de Sade and Mein Kampf, she changed her mousy brown hair to the peroxide blonde she is better known for and using a bright crimson lipstick.

The dowdy, cover all clothes were replaced with mini skirts, waistcoats, long, high heeled black boots to look more Germanic for him. Myra was so smitten with Ian she kept a diary and on every page started with "I hope Ian and I love each other all our lives". She became more involved in his world adopting the anti-social behaviour, and also, still being ignored by Ian.

Even at this early stage long before they were to become a couple Myra knew that Ian had a cruel side to his character which later would terrify her, she wrote a letter to a friend saying that if she were ever found dead, then go to the police and tell them that Brady is somehow involved.

In another letter many years later she reflected on this time and wrote, "Within months, he had convinced me that there was no God at all: he could have told me that the earth was flat, the moon was made of green cheese and the sun rose in the west, I would have believed him, such was his power of persuasion."

Ian's input into Myra's mindset went on for nearly a year, building her fascination with him and deepening her romantic hopes. It was not until December 22nd at the work's Christmas party that year that Ian asked Myra out to go to the cinema with him to see Judgement at Nuremberg. Of course, she was thrilled and giddy at the idea all her dreams were coming true.

Little did she know a nightmare was just beginning and this date would lead to Myra becoming an iconic symbol of pure evil. Even many decades later her eerie mugshot is often emblazoned on tabloid newspapers and her crimes still evoke national disgust and interest.

Myra's Change of Life with Ian Brady

At that fateful office Christmas party of December 1961 where Myra thought her dreams were coming true with the invitation to the cinema from Ian Brady, little did she know that was the start of the end as life as she knew it.

Myra swallowed all the Aryan propaganda and even admits to carrying around a photo of Irma Grese (a female SS guard at Auschwitz and Ravensbrück concentration camps) in her handbag. Ian now had her in his sights, he knew he could lead her into a life she had never dreamt of, but he had. He started calling her Hessie, a nickname in homage to Rudolph Hess.

He had also managed isolated her from friends, though at the time she was the one alienating them with her extreme views and anti-social behaviour, she only wanted to please Ian continually. In her mind his word was law and her life would not exist without him, by now she was totally besotted.

Now was the time he started to share his sexual and violent fantasies with Myra, although she did not want to hold back, some of her deep seated beliefs and morality still held her. This also, I have to say is where both of their accounts over all of the decades to follow deviate and change various times.

I think, that Ian was already into pornography and relished the idea of making his own pornographic pictures, Myra was not at this time so keen, but wanted to please Ian and in my point of view once she had started to open up for herself, she was a willing and even keen participant.

Myra was still at this time living with her grandmother, so when her grandmother went to bed, Ian brought into the small sitting room his camera and tripod, they stripped off and put hoods on their heads with just slits for eyes.

With a time delay device Ian took a series of about 30 pictures of them together having sex and of them individually posing. This may be seen as pretty tame by today's standards, in the 60s there was a market for this and they made some quick money.

Were they both thinking this was a way to make some easy money, or was it a control factor for Ian? Again, both parties have differing stories, Myra on many occasions said she was drunk or drugged by Ian to take these photos, he says she happily participated.
There was one contentious picture where it was seen that Myra had what seemed whip marks across her back and buttocks, Ian stated these were drawn on her body for the camera effects. In later years, Myra always claimed she was forced into it all and found it repulsive. For her appeals she would use this as grounds for parole saying Ian threatened to blackmail her with the intimate photos. Again, just my point of view on this, if the pictures had already been sold out in the public domain and Myra knew about this, why would he be able to blackmail her?

However, there is no doubt that this early dalliance with deviant sexualised photography was a gateway for the horrendous and heinous photos and tape recordings of their sexual assaults, torture and ultimate killings of their young victims later on.

Here, I think it is worth saying that without any doubt

the concept of these murders lie totally with Ian Brady, his warped perception of the true beliefs and theories, added to his deep seated need to prove he was different from the normal run of the mill person, were fuelled by the idealisation of him by Myra. She encouraged him to fulfil his fantasies and without a doubt she enabled them, none more so than by the procurement of the youngsters.

Without her active involvement, it is possible Pauline Reade, John Kilbride, Keith Bennett, Lesley Ann Downey and Edward Evans would have made it to adulthood instead of being murder victims?

That is a question that neither Myra nor Ian have answered.

There is without doubt various sides to this story and it has been changing over the years, trying to unravel it often depends on what side of the fence you are sitting, both Myra and Ian had people working for their freedom over the years.

But we have jumped forward because these killings came after other plotting. Ian had moved into Myra's grandmother's house in June 63.

Initially they were discussing and planning bank robberies together, Myra was persuaded by Ian to learn to drive, to be his getaway driver, until July 1963, when the talk deviated into child sexual abuse, abduction and their fantasy of "the perfect murder." Discussions over cheap wine, trips out in their minivan and experimentation with sexual sadism, launched their plot.

Accounts of all the murders vary from both Myra and Ian, so the facts are:

Both Myra and Ian had discussed what was going to happen to their victims, they had both decided on the 12th July as their first kill date.

Pauline Reade, was 16, the couple's first victim. Pauline was a neighbour of Myra's, so they knew each other. She was on her way to a local dance when Myra persuaded her to get in her car to go and help her find a lost glove. She drove Pauline to Saddleworth Moor where she was stripped, violated, beaten and stabbed.

Myra says: that Ian chose the victim and she was waiting in their mini-van, he flashed his lights on his motorbike to tell Myra who to get into the car. Also, Ian stripped, raped, tortured and killed Pauline. While she sat for 20 mins in the car.

Ian says: Myra picked out Pauline herself and got her into the car, he was still at home getting ready for the kill.

Ian drove to Saddleworth Moor on his motorbike, after the 2 had gone there together, he says it was Myra who stripped, violated Pauline, beat her and stabbed her several times, but had not killed her. He says he stepped in to finish it off.

Myra had thought that the killing of Pauline would bring her and Ian closer with such a shared experience, but he chose to explore his homosexual side and Myra says she felt pushed away. She embarked on an affair with a police man which Ian was rather amused about, but it also showed that she had ample opportunity to get out or come clean to him after just one killing, but she chose not to.

John Kilbride, aged 12, was snatched from Ashton market on Saturday November 23, 1963. He was strangled and buried in a shallow grave. Just four months later he was the second of Ian's and Myra's five victims.

Myra says: they (she and Ian) took this victim together, with the same glove story. Ian tried to cut his throat, but failed and then strangled him. All of this was done while she waited in the car.

Ian says: they did take the boy together, but both of them were involved in the sexual abuse and strangulation of John. Myra held him down during it all.

There are photographs of both Myra and Ian in the locations of the graves of both Pauline and John, they revisited the sites on numerous occasions.

Keith Bennett, also 12, faced a similar fate on the moors in June 1964, although this time there was no photographic evidence to assist in locating his grave, which has never been found and the method of killing him has never been confirmed.

Myra says: Ian sexually abused and killed Keith. Ian says: Myra held the boy down, just as the other times.

Ian was by now taking more photographs of their victims and trophies, these later would be part of their downfall.

In September 1964 the council moved Ellen Maybury (Myra's grandmother) into a new house 16 Wardle Brook Avenue, Hyde, Manchester. Myra and Ian moved in too.

Their 4th victim 10-year-old Lesley Ann Downey, who is in my mind probably the one most people remember and probably the victim that sealed the fates of both Myra and Ian when they came to court.

Lesley Ann was taken from a funfair just 200 yards from her home, on the 26th December, 1964 back to their home, she was brutally sexually abused, tortured and killed, this time no testimony was needed as Ian took multiple photos with both himself and Myra posting with the dead body and recorded the last sickening 16 mins of Lesley Ann's life with her pleading and screaming for her life and both Myra and Ian are clearly heard to being present and participating in her suffering and demise.

Though originally Myra said she did not know Lesley Ann was killed because she went out to run a bath. Later she did recant this statement. Also, Lesley Ann's body was in the house for quite a while, they were in no rush to move it and both recall, having sex, drinking whiskey and celebrating their sacrifice before falling asleep on the sofa.

It was snowy when they made the trip with Lesley Ann's body wrapped in a sheet in the boot of the car to Hollin Brown Knoll, a familiar place for both Ian and Myra. It was the first time that their victim had not walked onto the Moor, so Ian had to leave Myra and Lesley Ann in the car while he dug a shallow grave not far from Pauline Reade.

While he was out of sight digging a police car pulled up alongside Myra in the lay-by to ask if she was ok. Calmly she told the officer that the spark plugs were wet and she was letting them dry out and she was fine. The officer accepted this and drove off.

Again, Lesley Ann's body was buried on the Moor, along with photographic evidence. They went back to the house and cleaned up together before Myra went to collect her grandmother from a relative's home and bring her back to the house as if nothing had happened.

There is more photographic evidence that they both went back to Lesley Ann's grave time and time again capturing their visits with smiling happy photos.

By now Myra and Ian had been together 3 years and committed 4 murders, where and how would it end?

As 1965 started, Ian and Myra seemed to be starting new as well, Ian sold his bike and Myra sold her car, and bought a Mini Clubman, they were developing their original bank robbery plans, with the money Myra bought two guns, a Webley 45 and a Smith & Wesson 38, Ian loved to practice shooting on the Moors.

The few social connections Myra and Ian had was her younger sister Maureen and her husband David Smith. David had been in trouble with the police at a young age, aggression (actual bodily harm) and minor theft (house breaking), but recently he and Maureen had suffered the unexpected death of their baby daughter.

David was drinking more and vocal about wanting to change his life, Ian saw this as an opportunity to engage him in their bank robbery plot. Even though David had seen and shot both guns on the Moors, he had said that he did not want to use live ammunition in the robbery, Ian was insistent on this matter.

Edward Evans, at 17, was the sick duo's fifth and final victim. He had just been to see Manchester United play when Brady lured in Edward. Brady repeatedly bludgeoned Evans with an axe

Myra had driven Ian to Manchester Central railway station on the evening of the 6th October, 1965 to pick a young man to have sex with.

Manchester United had been playing, so there were many young men out that evening. She says Ian returned to the car with 17 year old Edward Evans and she drove them all back to their home in Hyde.

During the evening there was plenty of alcohol, music, conversation. Ian sent Myra out to fetch her brother-in-law David to their house. Myra visited her sister and asked David to walk her back as she did not like walking alone on a dark night, when they arrived at her house, she invited him in for some wine.

David was drinking in the kitchen when Myra called him into the lounge after he had heard a loud bang. He went into the lounge to see Ian holding Edward up and Myra watching, Ian dropped the young man onto the floor and hit him repeatedly with an axe before strangling him.

Myra busy cleaning up, making tea, joking and laughing, she got David to help her. They rolled

Edward's body into a plastic sheet and placed it in the spare bedroom.

David was also just 17 at the time and so scared that the same was going to happen to him. As soon as he left that evening, he went home and then to the police to report what had happened.

The police came to the house on the morning of the 7th October, 1965, the body of Edward was still there along with the axe, Ian was arrested immediately. Myra was not arrested until the 11th October, because the idea of a woman abducting and killing children went against the very notion of womanhood and the police did not arrest Myra until there was overwhelming evidence of her complicity.

During the days between the 7th and 11th October, Myra did her best to destroy a lot of damming evidence, but not all and that would add to the horrific story that was still to unfold.

The Arrest and Comital of Myra Hindley and Ian Brady.

David Smith was just 17 years old and terrified when he left Ian Brady and Myra Hindley at their home at 3.00 am on the 7th October, 1965. He had just witnessed the mutilation and death of another 17 year old Edward Evans at the brutal hands of

Ian, so much so he had sprained his ankle, along with the callous clean up of Myra.

He had agreed to return with his baby's pram in the morning to move the body from the house to the car to then bury Edward like the others on the Moors.

David ran home to Maureen horrified, sickened and scared. He had a cup of tea, was physically sick and then told Maureen what he had seen. He waited until the just after 6.00 am for daylight, armed himself with a screwdriver and bread knife, in case Ian or Myra tried to attack him, he went to the local phone box and called the police. A car was sent to collect him and he was taken to Hyde police station, where he told the officers everything that had happened the previous evening.

Superintendent Bob Talbot of the Stalybridge police division went to Wardle Brook Avenue, accompanied by other detectives. He wore the overall of a bread deliveryman on top of his uniform to avoid any initial suspicion.

He knocked the back door and asked Myra if her husband was home. She denied having a husband or that a man was in the house, Talbot then identified himself. Myra led him into the living room, to find Ian lying on a bed, writing to his employer about his ankle injury. Talbot explained that he was investigating "an act of violence involving guns" that was reported to have taken place the previous evening Myra denied to him that there had been any violence, he was then joined by other officers and the police were allowed to look around the house.

When police asked for the key to the locked spare bedroom, she said it was at her workplace; but when the police offered to take her to work to retrieve it, Ian told her to hand it over. After seeing the dead body of. Young man wrapped in plastic and a bloody axe in the room the officers returned to the living room they arrested Brady on suspicion of murder. As Brady was getting dressed, he said, "Eddie and I had a row and the situation got out of hand."

Myra was not initially arrested, but she demanded to go with Ian to the police station, also taking her dog. She refused to make any statement about Edward's death except saying it had been an accident and was allowed to go home on the condition that she return the next day. Over the next four days Myra visited her employer and asked to be dismissed, on one of these occasions, she found an envelope belonging to Ian which she burned in an ashtray; she said that she did not open it but believed it contained their plans for bank robberies. On 11 October, she too was arrested and taken into custody, being charged as an accessory to the murder of Edward and was remanded at HM Prison Risley.

Police searching their house found an old exercise book with the name "John Kilbride", which made them suspect that Ian and Myra had been involved in the disappearances of other youngsters. Ian told police that he and Edward had fought but insisted that he and Smith had murdered Evans and that Myra had "only done what she had been told".

David said that Ian packed notebooks and photos into suitcases; he had no idea what else the suitcases contained or where they might be, though he mentioned that Ian "had a thing about railway stations". A search of left-luggage offices turned up the suitcases at Manchester Central railway station on 15 October; the claim ticket was later found in Myra's prayer book.

Inside one of the cases were a various assortment of costumes, notes, photographs and negatives, nine pornographic photographs taken of Lesley Ann Downey, naked and with a scarf tied across her mouth, and a sixteen- minute audiotape recording of a girl identifying herself as Lesley Ann screaming, crying, and pleading to be allowed to return home to her mother. Lesley Ann Downey's mother later confirmed that the recording, was of her daughter.

From information given in a local house to house investigation, they obtained details of areas that Ian and Myra used to like to visit on the Moor. On the 16 October an arm bone was found protruding from the peat, which was presumed at first to be Kilbride's, but which the next day was identified as that of Lesley Ann Downey, whose body was still visually identifiable; her mother was able to identify the clothing which had also been buried in the grave.

In a photograph taken by Ian in November 1963, Myra crouches over John Kilbride's grave on Saddleworth Moor with her dog, Puppet.

Also among the photographs in the suitcase were a number of scenes of the moors. David told police that Ian had boasted of "photographic proof" of multiple murders, and officers, struck by Ian's decision to remove the apparently innocent landscapes from their house, an appeal for help to find locations in the photographs.

On 21 October they found the badly decomposed body of John Kilbride, which had to be identified by clothing. That same day, already being held for the murder of Edward, Ian and Myra appeared at Hyde Magistrates' Court charged with Lesley Ann Downey's
murder. Ian and Myra were brought before the court separately and remanded into custody for a week. They made a two-minute appearance on 28th October and were again remanded into custody.

The investigating officers suspected Ian and Myra of murdering other missing children and teenagers who had disappeared from areas in and around Manchester over the previous few years, and the search for bodies continued after the discovery of Kilbride's body, but with winter setting in it was called off in November.

Presented with the evidence of the tape recording, Ian admitted to taking the photographs of Lesley Ann Downey, by 2 December, Ian had been charged with the murders of John Kilbride, Lesley Ann Downey and Edward Evans.

Myra had been charged with the murders of Lesley Ann Downey and Edward Evans and being an accessory to the murder of John Kilbride.

At the further committal hearing on the 6th December, Ian was charged with the murders of Edward Evans, John Kilbride, and Lesley Ann Downey, and Myra with the murders of Edward Evans and Lesley Ann Downey, as well as with harbouring Ian in the knowledge that he had killed John Kilbride.

The proceedings continued before three magistrates in Hyde over an eleven-day period during December, at the end of which the pair were committed for trial at Chester Assizes.

Many of the photographs taken by Ian and Myra on the moor featured Myra's dog Puppet, sometimes as a puppy. To help date the photos, detectives had a veterinary surgeon examine the dog to determine his age; the examination required a general anaesthetic from which Puppet did not recover. Myra was furious and accused the police of murdering the dog, one of the few occasions detectives witnessed any emotional response from her. Myra wrote to her mother:

"I feel as though my heart's been torn to pieces. I don't think anything could hurt me more than this has. The only consolation is that some moron might have got hold of Puppet and hurt him."

However, the show, the stories and national as well a global captivation of people was just starting.

The Trial of the Century Hindley & Brady

The fourteen-day trial, before Justice Fenton Atkinson, began on 19 April 1966. The courtroom was fitted with security screens to protect Ian Brady and Myra Hindley who were charged with murdering Edward Evans, Lesley Ann Downey and John Kilbride. The Attorney General, Sir Elwyn Jones, led the prosecution, assisted by William Mars-Jones. Ian Brady was defended by Emlyn Hooson QC and Myra Hindley was defended by Godfrey Heilpern QC.

In preparation of this momentous trial with global media interest, both Ian and Myra had been given the same lawyer, which meant they could meet up, pass messages to each other and have time together.

David Smith was the chief prosecution witness.

However, the News of the World had offered him £1,000 for his story and much was made of this by the defense in court, trying to discredit him, but the judge ruled that the involvement of the newspaper had be untimely and inconsiderate, but with all the statements David had given to the police prior to this offer made it irrelevant.

Both Ian and Myra entered pleas of not guilty, Ian testified for over eight hours, Myra for six. Ian admitted to striking Edward with the axe, but claimed that someone else had killed Evans, pointing to the pathologist's statement that his death had been "accelerated by strangulation"; Ian's "calm, undisguised arrogance did not help him to win the jury over. Myra denied any knowledge that the photographs of Saddleworth Moor found by police had been taken near the graves of their victims.

The sixteen-minute tape recording of Lesley Ann Downey, on which the voices of Ian and Myra were audible, was played in open court. Myra admitted that her attitude towards Lesley Ann Downey was brusque and cruel, but claimed that was only because she was afraid that someone might hear her screaming. Myra claimed that when Lesley Ann was being undressed, she was downstairs; when the pornographic photographs were taken, she was looking out the window; and that when Lesley Ann was being strangled, she was running a bath.

On 6 May, after having deliberated for a little over

two hours, the jury found Ian guilty of all three murders, and Myra guilty of the murders of Lesley Ann Downey and Edward Evans. The death penalty for murder had been abolished while Ian and Myra were held on remand, the judge passed the only sentence that the law allowed: life imprisonment. Ian Brady was sentenced to three concurrent life sentences and Myra Hindley was given two, plus a concurrent seven-year term for harbouring Ian Brady in the knowledge that he had murdered John Kilbride. Ian Brady was taken to HM Prison Durham and Myra Hindley was sent to HM Prison Holloway.

In his closing remarks, Atkinson described the murders as "truly horrible" and the accused as "two sadistic killers of the utmost depravity", he recommended they spend "a very long time" in prison before being considered for parole, but did not stipulate a tariff. He called Ian "wicked beyond belief" and said he saw no reasonable possibility of reform for him, though he did not think the same necessarily true of Myra once "removed from Brady's influence". Throughout the trial Ian Brady and Myra Hindley "stuck rigidly to their strategy of lying", and Myra Hindley was later described as "a quiet, controlled, impassive witness who lied remorselessly".

This story does not end here, in fact, it is just the beginning of a lifelong story for both Ian and Myra that has many twists, turns and media coverage. Their life behind bars is a whole new story.

For most convicted serial killers, the public and media interest in their intrigue and story ends with their conviction, not so with Myra Hindley and Ian Brady, more twists and turns follow them for over many decades.

As soon as they were convicted Myra lodged and appeal, which she lost, even though to her end she believed she would be freed and was prepared to manipulate and adapt her story to that end. However, Ian was much more committed to his version of events.

On conviction Myra was sent to HMP Holloway, in London, for a long time it was the largest female prison in Western Europe, it has a fascinating and gruesome history with numerous infamous inmates within its walls.

From May 6th, 1966, Myra continually, regularly corresponded with Ian by letter unto 1971 when she ended their relationship. Myra and Ian exchanged letters for a few months after, but Myra says she had fallen in love with Patricia Cairn, a prison guard in Holloway prison. Relationships like this are not unusual.

Myra successfully petitioned to get her Category A prisoner status changed to a B, so that opened up the options for external walks on Hampstead Heath with the Governor, the national press picked this up and there was a huge public outcry. With the help of Patricia Cairns and outside support from another prisoner, Myra planned a prison escape, luckily the impressions of the prison keys were discovered by an off duty police officer. Patricia received a six year jail sentence for her part in the plot and Myra was told that she would serve twenty five years before being eligible for parole, in 1985 the Home Secretary Leon Brittan increased that to thirty years. Margaret Thatcher told Leon Brittan "His proposed minimum sentences of thirty years for Hindley and forty years for Brady were too short," saying, "I do not think that either of these prisoners should ever be released from custody.

Their crime was the most hideous and cruel in modern times."

After numerous appeals for parole which were always denied, in 1987 Myra admitted that most of her evidence for her parole hearings had been lies. Even her co-operation whilst at HMP Cookham Wood and trips to the Moors to work with police to find the two graves of Pauline Reade and Keith Bennett. Pauline Reade's grave was found in 1987 through evidence given by Ian Brady. In 1990 Myra admitted to being more involved in the killings and procurement of the victims, so the Home Secretary David Waddington imposed a full life tariff on her, however she was not informed of this change until 1994, when the Law Lords changed the requirements to inform all prisoners with life tariffs.

In early 1998 Myra was moved to the medium-security HM Prison Highpoint, the House of Lords ruling left open the possibility of later freedom. Between December 1997 and March 2000, Myra made three separate appeals against her life tariff, claiming she was a reformed woman and no longer a danger to society, she had returned to religion, but each was rejected by the courts.

In 2002 it was challenged that the judges not the politicians had the authority to sentence prisoners, on the 25th November it was changed, which meant any prisoner that had been sentenced by a politician could appeal and possibly be freed. Something Myra had wanted.

However, she has missed the death penally by weeks back in 1965, she also missed this possibility by 10 days, Myra died at 60 on the 15th November, 2002, a chain smoker, she died from bronchial pneumonia at West Suffolk Hospital. The intense horror and public disgust after 37 years of her crimes was still so intense that 20 local undertakers refused to manage her cremation and there were 8 people at her funeral, none of which were family members. Her ashes were taken and spread by Patricia Cairns.

Now, nearly another two decades after her death, people are still intrigued by this blonde haired, everyday girl who became the most evil woman in Britain. In my mind, I have no doubt that Ian Brady was at first the master and the teacher, but like in so many cases the pupil out learns the teacher. It is known that Myra can be manipulative, calculating and demanding, her story has changed many times over the years, maybe she convinced herself they were her truths. She had many opportunities to tell people where the other grave of Keith Bennett was, but she never did.

Rose West
Rosemarie Letts Morphed into Rose West, The Most Deviant Woman in Britain

Rosemarie Letts was just 15 when she met Fred West, but from even before birth she had not had it easy. Her mother Daisy had suffered with severe depression during the pregnancy and as was the way in 1953 in Devon, part of her treatment was electroconvulsive therapy, this may have left a substantial permanent psychological effect on Rosemarie.

From a very early age she witnessed the physical and emotional brutality of her father William towards her mother, he had returned from the war with mental health issues. He continually bullied, bashed and berated his wife Daisy, Rosemarie and her 6 siblings.

As Rose started to develop into her teenage years, she became highly sexually active as well as displaying signs that she needed help, like walking around the family home naked and fondling her younger brother in bed. Her father as well as physically abusive, forbade her to date boys of her own age, so Rose started to be very promiscuous with much older men. Daisy downtrodden and abused for years, saw this and with great courage took Rose and left the family home. Rose however, soon moved back and in the same year 1969, she met Fred West at a Cheltenham bus stop shortly after her 15th birthday, he was 27.

Although Rose had a deviant and difficult relationship with her father, both of her parents tried in vain to convince her to end this relationship with Fred. Her father had sexually abused Rose, some say he was jealous, but with both Fred and Rose having difficult childhoods, this built a bond. William took 15 year old Rose to Social Services to get her away from Fred, but they let her keep in touch with him up to her 16th birthday when she was legally old enough to choose for herself and she chose to live with Fred.

Fred was still married to his first wife Catherine Costello when he met Rosemary, but she left her job and moved in with him and cared for his two daughters Charmaine and Anne Marie. A lot to take on at just 16, Charmaine did not like, or get on with Rose, she was an unruly and difficult child and a lot of evidence came to light later on that Rose continually, severely punished Charmaine.

In 1971, while Fred was in jail for ten months for

dishonesty offences, eight-year-old Charmaine disappeared. Rosemarie claimed that Charmaine had gone to live with her mother. Charmaine's remains were found in 1994 at 25 Midland Road, where the couple lived at the time. The previous year, Catherine Costello, Charmaine's mother, had also disappeared. In March 1970, the 25 year old vanished, though the police weren't notified. Catherine's family heard that she'd moved to Saudi Arabia, but her remains were found in 1994.

Evidence shows that Rose was already earning money as a prostitute at Midland Road, with a very young baby and two young children to care for alone at the age of 17.

United again Rose and Fred move to 25 Cromwell Street, Gloucester, a place that was to become known as the House of Horrors and still today is synonymous with the Wests. They moved into this house early 1971 just after they had secretly married. Then their macabre fantasies came to life.

30 Years On. Reflecting on the Arrest of Fred West and the Lingering Legacy of their Crimes

Thirty years have passed since the arrest of Fred West, a name synonymous with horror, depravity, and the darkest corners of the human psyche.

At 11.15 am on the 25th February, 1994 Fred confessed to the manslaughter of his daughter, Heather. This was just the start of uncovering his crimes, committed alongside his wife Rosemarie West, which shocked the world and left an indelible mark on society. As we mark this grim anniversary, it's an opportune moment to reflect on the legacy of their atrocities and the enduring impact they have had on criminal psychology, law enforcement, and society as a whole.

The Genesis of Horror: The story of Fred and Rosemary West, is one that defies comprehension. Operating from their seemingly ordinary home in Gloucester, they embarked on a reign of terror that claimed the lives of at least twelve young women and girls. Their victims, many of whom were subjected to unspeakable acts of torture and abuse, were buried in the garden and cellar of their residence, transforming the house of horrors into a symbol of unimaginable evil.

The Shockwaves of Discovery: The revelation of the crimes committed by both Fred and Rose West sent shockwaves through the community and beyond. It shattered the illusion of safety and forced society to confront the uncomfortable reality that monsters can lurk behind the most ordinary façades. The subsequent investigation unearthed a web of deception, manipulation, and psychological torment, shedding light on the complexities of criminal behaviour and the dynamics of abusive relationships. Both Fred and Rose were sexual sadists and murderers, in their own right, the torture and exploitation of vulnerable females, including their own daughters came easily to them.

A Turning Point in Criminal Psychology: The case of Fred and Rosemary West prompted a paradigm shift in the field of criminal psychology. It highlighted the importance of understanding the interplay between individual pathology, environmental factors, and social dynamics in the commission of heinous crimes. Psychologists and criminologists delved into the psyche of the perpetrators, seeking to unravel the twisted motivations and distorted perceptions that drove their actions.

Lessons Learned: The legacy of their crimes extends far beyond the confines of a courtroom. It serves as a stark reminder of the need for vigilance, empathy, and proactive intervention in cases of domestic abuse and violence. Their story underscores the importance of listening to victims, believing their accounts, and providing them with the support and resources they need to break free from cycles of abuse.

The Pursuit of Justice: While Fred West ultimately evaded facing trial for his crimes by taking his own life, the quest for justice for the victims and their families continues to this day. The legacy of the

Wests serves as a catalyst for ongoing efforts to improve law enforcement practices, enhance victim support services, and strengthen legal frameworks to prevent similar tragedies from occurring in the future.

Conclusion: Thirty years on from the arrest of Fred West and later on Rose West, the wounds inflicted by their crimes still run deep. Yet, amidst the darkness, there are glimmers of hope. The legacy of the Wests serves as a sobering reminder of the capacity for evil that resides within humanity, but also as a testament to the resilience of the human spirit and the enduring pursuit of justice and healing. As we reflect on this grim anniversary, let us reaffirm our commitment to confronting evil, supporting victims, and striving for a world where such horrors are consigned to the annals of history.

Marie-Therese Kouao and her boyfriend, Carl Manning

On the 25th February 2000, the United Kingdom was shaken by a horrific case of child abuse that would forever change the landscape of child protection. The victim, an innocent eight-year-old girl named Victoria

Climbié, suffered unimaginable cruelty at the hands of those entrusted with her care.

Background: Victoria Climbié was born in the Ivory Coast and brought to England by her great- aunt Marie-Thérèse Kouao. Instead of finding safety and care, Victoria fell victim to relentless abuse and neglect, she was beaten with bicycle chains and kept trussed up in a plastic sack in an unlit, unheated bathroom. Over the course of several months, with two hospital visits, she endured physical, emotional, and psychological torment, leaving her in a state of extreme vulnerability.

Failure of the System: The tragedy of Victoria Climbié's murder was compounded by the failure of the child protection system. Despite numerous opportunities for intervention, social services, healthcare professionals, and the police were unable to prevent the escalating abuse. This case highlighted some critical shortcomings in communication and collaboration among various agencies responsible for safeguarding children.

Impact and Reforms: The shockwaves of Victoria's death prompted a national outcry for reform. The ensuing inquiry, led by Lord Laming, uncovered systemic failures in child protection.

The Climbié case became a catalyst for significant changes in policies and procedures, leading to the establishment of the Every Child Matters initiative. This initiative aimed to improve coordination between agencies, prioritise the welfare of the child and enhance training for professionals involved in child protection.

Legacy: Victoria Climbié's legacy is one of tragedy, but also of transformation. Her case exposed the dire need for a more robust and integrated approach to child welfare. The changes implemented in the wake of her death aimed to prevent such a failure of protection from occurring again.

Conclusion: The murder of Victoria Climbié is a painful chapter in the history of child protection in the UK. However, through the reforms that followed, her story became a catalyst for positive change. As we remember Victoria, we must also strive to maintain and strengthen our commitment to protecting the most vulnerable members of our society.

Unfortunately, it was not the last child murder that would shock the nation, Peter Connelly, 17 month old infant who was found dead in his family home in Haringey. His mother, stepfather and uncle were all convicted of his murder.

Arthur Lambinjo-Hughes, was just 6 when he was murdered during Covid lockdown on 16 June 2020 by his stepmother and father.

Decades after Victoria's horrific death, our children

are still at risk with parents in toxic relationships and a welfare system stretched to breaking point.

No child deserves to die as Victoria, Peter or Arthur have done, there have been others too.

Lucy Letby

Lucy Letby's refusal to return to court to hear the jury's outcome and also face the findings of the jury in her case likely stems from a combination of psychological, emotional, and legal factors. It's important to note that the following analysis is speculative and based on general psychological principles, as I don't have access to specific details about her case beyond what was publicly known.

Denial and Disbelief:
One of the primary psychological mechanisms that might contribute to Letby's refusal to want to hear and accept the jury's findings is denial. Facing the reality of being found guilty of such serious charges can be overwhelming and emotionally distressing. Denial is a defense mechanism that the mind employs to protect itself from painful truths. In Letby's case, she might find it incredibly difficult to accept the idea that her actions led to the tragic deaths of infants she was meant to care for.

Self-Preservation and Identity:
Being found guilty can shatter an individual's self-image and identity. For Letby, who was regarded as a compassionate nurse dedicated to caring for children, accepting her guilt could mean dismantling her self-concept and facing the fact that she is now seen as someone entirely different. This threat to her sense of self could be a powerful psychological barrier to accepting the jury's verdict.

Psychological Dissonance:
If Letby truly believes she is innocent, there would be a cognitive dissonance between her self-perception and the jury's findings. This dissonance can cause extreme discomfort, leading her to reject the verdict to maintain internal psychological harmony.

Legal Strategy:
In some cases, individuals facing legal consequences might refuse to accept a guilty verdict as part of a legal strategy. This could possibly be linked to an appeal process or a hope for a reduced sentence. Llegal considerations can heavily influence an individual's behaviour during and after a trial.

Emotional Coping:
The emotional toll of facing a guilty verdict can be immense. Refusing to accept the findings could be a way for Letby to shield herself from the emotional pain and guilt associated with her alleged actions. By not acknowledging the verdict, she may be attempting to distance herself emotionally from the

reality of the situation.

Hope for Reversal:

Letby's refusal to accept the jury's findings could also be driven by a deep-seated hope that her situation will eventually change. She might be banking on the possibility of new evidence emerging, legal appeals succeeding, or public sentiment shifting in her favour. This hope could serve as a psychological defense against the harsh reality she faces.

In conclusion:

Lucy Letby's refusal to return to court to hear and accept the jury's findings likely stems from a complex interplay of psychological, emotional, and legal factors. Denial, self-preservation, psychological dissonance, legal strategy, emotional coping, and hope for reversal could all contribute to her stance. While these speculations may provide some insight, understanding her specific mindset would require a thorough analysis by mental health professionals and legal experts, which is beyond the scope of general speculation.

True Crime People & Places

Part 3

Children Who Kill:

James Fairweather The 15 year old serial killer that terrified Colchester in 2014.

James Fairweather was just 15 when he brutally stabbed to death father of five, 33 year old James Attfield, who was laying on the grass in a park in Colchester on the sunny 29th March, 2014.

James Attfield previously had survived a terrific car accident that had damaged his brain. As he lay quietly in Castle Park Fairweather ferociously attacked him, as a random stranger Fairweather's victim could have been anyone. At his trial Fairweather had said that voices had chosen Attfield and were laughing while he was stabbing his victim.

When the paramedics arrived in the park James Attfield was bleeding to death, with over 100 stab wounds, they could not save him. All the cuts and wounds to his hands and arms showed that he had been able to put up a fight with Fairweather, but the attack was just too frenzied. During the trail of James Fairweather the BBC deemed the very disturbing degree of injuries were too gruesome to describe in any news coverage.

His second victim, Almanea, a mature student at Essex university was viciously stabbed and killed on the 17th June, in an over grown area very close to her home. There were stab wounds her in her stomach, through her eyes and others into her brain.

Because these two victims were not known to each other, or connected to Fairweather the investigation was slow and hard, the attacks were at different times of the day and the victims' different genders, different ethnic backgrounds, one was committed in an open public space and the other in a more secluded area, but close to a public footpath, so all the usual profiling parameters were not useful.

Over 900 suspects were interviewed from Essex and East Anglia, Colchester Council and private residents cleared overgrowth in public areas to remove hiding places, fewer people went out in the town.

Fairweather, waited over a year before he was ready to attack again, because of the heightened public awareness of danger, on the 27th May, 2015, he was seen hanging about early in the morning by a wary dog walker. The police were called and they found Fairweather wearing rubber gloves and with a knife, he was arrested, during the investigation his plans to murder 15 people came to light.

Subsequently, Fairweather was assessed by four

psychiatrists to be on the Autism Spectrum, but not psychotic as Fairweather claimed to be. He was found unanimously guilty by the jury on the 22nd April, 2016. Fairweather was sentenced to life imprisonment with a minimum of 27 years.

There was an appeal, which was rejected and the sentence upheld.

The onerous title of the youngest double murderers in the UK, at just goes to two 14 year olds from Spalding, Kim Edwards and her boyfriend Lucas Markham.

Killing is most often a singular occupation, there have been a few notorious killing couples, Myra Hindley and Ian Brady, Rose & Fred West, Amanda Badges and David Lehane in the UK, but none more callous and calculating than Kim and Lucas.

Kim felt shut out by her mum and younger sister, tensions, arguments and resentments had been growing since 2008 when Kim was just 6 years old. Elizabeth Edwards (mum) had searched for help from Social Services, her GP and CAMHS for Kim and for family therapy, it seemed to have various highs and lows until Kim met Lucas and a major divide set in.

Lucas was banned from the house, so they met in the garden. Their murderous plotting started in the playground, but when Lucas was excluded from school, they carried on devising their plan at McDonalds and his home.

The night that Elizabeth and Katie were viciously stabbed to death in their beds, was not Lucas's first attempt, in fact it was the third, on two previous arranged dates Kim had fallen asleep and not let Lucas into the house through the bathroom window as arranged.

He came equipped with a bag of knives and both victims were brutally stabbed to death in their beds with pillows over their faces to muffle their screams.

If it were not barbaric enough that Kim had fallen asleep on two previous dates, with the two dead bodies in the bedrooms Kim and Lucas locked themselves in the house, had sex in the living room before snuggling up to watch TV with snacks. They kept this up for two days, they ignored neighbours and police calling at the house.

When the police broke into the house, they found Kim and Lucas calmly on the sofa together. When the police asked about her mother and sister, their response was "look upstairs."

The lack of emotion, remorse and disinterest

shocked seasoned professionals, Kim was assessed psychologically, but no disorders could be found, she clearly stated she hated her mother.

They were both shielded by the courts at first and their names could not be made public, but because of the heinous nature of the crimes and the response from both perpetrators, the ban was lifted.

Edwards and Markham were originally jailed for at least 20 years each, but judges have reduced the sentences to 17 and a half years.

On their release they may still be young enough and able to have a life of their own, but could you imagine closing your eyes to sleep if either of them was your partner?

Part 4
Myth Busting:

Busting 6 Myths About Serial Killers

Myth 1: Serial Killers Are Dysfunctional Loners

The majority of serial killers are not reclusive, social misfits who live alone. They are not monsters and may not appear strange. Many serial killers hide in plain sight within their communities. Serial murderers often have families and homes, are gainfully employed, and appear to be normal members of the community. Many serial murderers can blend in so effortlessly, they are often at times overlooked by the police and the public.

Myth 2: Serial Killers Are All White Males

Contrary to popular belief, serial killers span all racial groups, genders and ages. The racial diversification of serial killers generally mirrors that of the overall population, however there are still significantly fewer women than men.

As well as murdering three people, the evil Peter Bryan proceeded to eat their brains.

Zahid Younis was locked up for 38 years after killing two women and hiding their bodies in a freezer.

Aman Vyas was dubbed the "E17 night stalker" after he turned a small area near his home in Walthamstow, East London, into his "hunting ground" jailed for life with a minimum term of 37 years for the rape of four women and murder of one.

Aaron McKenzie was jailed for killing his heavily pregnant girlfriend and their baby on June 29, 2019.

Danyal Hussein "butchered" two sisters to death after making a blood pact with a demon to "sacrifice women" in return for winning the lottery.

Myth 3: Serial Killers Are Only Motivated By Sex

All serial murders are not sexually based. There are many other motivations for serial murders including anger, thrill, financial gain, and attention seeking.

Myth 4: Serial Killers Operate in Wide Areas

Most serial killers have very defined geographic areas of operation. They conduct their killings within comfort zones that are often defined by an anchor point (e.g. place of residence, employment, or residence of a relative). Serial murderers will, at times, spiral their activities outside of their comfort zone, when their confidence has grown through experience, or to avoid detection. Very few serial murderers travel nationally to kill, however, there have been some killers that have relocated and started to kill in their new area and even rarer occasions a new country.

Myth 5: Serial Killers Are Insane or Evil Geniuses

Serial killers have either a debilitating mental

condition, or they are extremely clever and intelligent. As a group, serial killers suffer from a variety of personality disorders, including psychopathy, anti-social personality, and others. Most, however, are not adjudicated as insane under the law. Like other populations, serial killers range in intelligence from borderline to above average levels.

Myth 6: Serial Killers Want to Get Caught

Offenders committing a crime for the first time are inexperienced. They gain experience and confidence with each new offence, eventually succeeding with few mistakes or problems. While most serial killers plan their offences more thoroughly than other criminals, the learning curve is still very steep. They must select, target, approach, control, and dispose of their victims.

The logistics involved in committing a murder and disposing of the body can become very complex, especially when there are multiple sites involved.

As serial killers continue to offend without being captured, they can become empowered, feeling they will never be identified. As the series continues, the killers may begin to take shortcuts when committing their crimes. This often causes the killers to take more chances, leading to identification and detection by police. It is not that serial killers want to get caught; they feel that they can't get caught.

In my experience very few criminals feel any remorse, or guilt and lack empathy for their victims and the larger effect caused by their atrocious acts. Most are proud of their acts, relive events through their trophies and media coverage, all are manipulative and secretive.

True Crime People & Places

Part 5

Linda's Insights:

Criminal Profiling is Still an Art Rather than a Science.

What is the difference between a perpetrator's signature and their MO?

True and fictitious crimes are everywhere now for the public, series, films, documentaries, books, articles and podcast. All with easy access globally.

Often the use of a killer's MO (Modus Operandi) and signature are used and many people ask me what is the difference?

Both are important concepts and can be used

together, but not always. All perpetrators in any crime have their MO, where, when, how, who they target. For many the location is somewhere that feels safe, or a location they know well.

Inside a property or out in the open. When, also tells you about the agility of a killer, it is much easier to offend in the dark, getting away, less likelihood of being disturbed. How, stabbing, strangulation, kidnapping says a lot about the confidence and strength of the killer, a dead body weight even of a small person is very heavy and hard to move. Time constraints also demonstrate a lot, are they in and out quickly or not. The who, is often a key, there are similarities in their victims, most serial killers keep to one gender, most (not all) to a single ethnicity.

However, the actual choice is significant to them, but may be something as simple as a perfume, or the colour of their coat, which to an outsider does not seem significant, until you can compare it to other victims.

The MO can be similar to many people, but they all have different triggers, or reasons for killing, they are not always unique to one killer or serial attacker.

However, the signature is unique, this is where something will be deliberately left as an identification. Unfortunately, this cannot be distinguished with a single kill, there has to be a comparison.

You will often see the MO modifying, or becoming cleaner, just like any skills, the more you practice the better you become, serial killing or serial offending are the same. It is highly unlikely that the first offence will be perfect, so they will want to improve. The perpetrator will progress, refine their method as they grow in confidence, early offences often give some good insights.

Whereas, the signature will be present from the start, because it is a ritual unique to that perpetrator.

Not all serial killers, or serial violent offenders have specific signatures as such, but they will usually have traits and behaviours that are special to them. Whereas all criminals have their MO.

Profiling and detection use all these points and many more. It is time consuming and painstaking work to gather the details, behaviours and evidence together to find individuals and to be able to prosecute them successfully.

The concept of Criminal Profiling has many myths, and I am sure that all murder investigations, sexual assault cases and serial killer detective teams would love to solve all their cases in 60 or 90 mins as per the entertainment media shows. Alas, the reality is very different, a huge amount of time, effort and consideration go into any profile.

Investigative Psychology

A Forensic Psychologist will work with data and intuition, they will study offending behaviour before, during and after the crime.

Psychological profiling is described as a method of suspect identification which seeks to identify a person's mental, emotional and personality characteristics based on things done, or left at the crime scene. Details and data are crucial, the British way of working is based on scientific research and builds from the bottom up.

There are significant tells in the geographical choice of location for the offender, it is usually somewhere they know, have been, feel comfortable, or they commute to a location (away from their usual habitat) a Geographical Profiler will look into a location from a multitude of perspectives.

Access to transport: how would the perpetrator get to the scene, rail, road, bus, walking?

Location: How public is the offending area? What time of day was the crime committed?

Was the crime scene organised or disorganised - a calm or frenzied attack?

A disorganised offender is more likely to have committed the crime in a moment of passion. There will be little or no evidence of premeditation and they are more likely to leave evidence such as blood, semen, murder weapon etc. behind. This type of offender is thought to be less socially competent and more likely to be unemployed, or in lower skilled employment, often lives alone.

An organised offender leads an ordered life and kills after some sort of critical life event. Their actions are premeditated and planned, they are likely to bring weapons and restraints to the scene. They are likely to be of average to high intelligence and employed in a more killed occupation.

Were trophies taken?

How was the victim left, was the victim posed, left in the open or buried?

How the offender interacts with their victim often gives many details about how they interact with people in their everyday life.

Profiling is a tool, but not the be all and end all defense that TV and movie makers like to make it out to be.

Crime scene analysis, good evidence collection, photographs all work together to provide guidance.

Watching, comparing, revisiting, linking similarities and patience are all essential to profiling in any scenario.

Peter Allen, Gwynne Evans and Ruth Ellis were the last people hanged for murder in England.

The Murder (Abolition of Death Penalty) Act 1965 is an Act of Parliament of the United Kingdom which abolished the death penalty for murder in Great Britain (the death penalty for murder survived in Northern Ireland until 1973). The act replaced the penalty of death with a mandatory sentence of imprisonment for life.

The 1965 act replaced the Homicide Act 1957, which had already reduced hangings to only four or fewer per year. However, there were exceptions to the 1965 act which left four capital offences: high treason, "piracy with violence" (piracy with intent to kill or cause grievous bodily harm), arson in royal dockyards and espionage, as well as other capital offences under military law.

The legislation contained a sunset clause, which stated that the act would expire on 31 July 1970 "unless Parliament by affirmative resolutions of both Houses otherwise determines". Resolutions were passed in the Commons and Lords on 16 and 18 December 1969, thereby making the act permanent.

The death penalty was not fully abolished in the

United Kingdom until 1998 by the Human Rights Act and the Crime and Disorder Act.

The last people to hang for murder were: Ruth Ellis in Holloway Prison, London on the 13th July, 1955, aged 28.

Ruth was convicted for the murder of her lover David Blakely, she shot him on Easter Sunday, 10th April, outside the Magdala pub in north London.

The last men were hanged on 13 August 1964, Peter Allen at Walton Prison in Liverpool, and Gwynne Evans at Strangeways Prison in Manchester for murdering John Alan West during a theft four months earlier.

However, there was a public and media outcry to bring back capital punishment for Ian Brady and Myra Hindley when they were sentenced on the 6th May, 1965. The death penalty had been abolished whilst they were both incarcerated on remand.

PSYCHOPATHY VERSUS PSYCHOSIS

Some serial killers have been diagnosed by psychologists as psychopaths, suffering from an antisocial personality disorder (APD) very few have been identified as criminally insane.

This makes them unlikely to conform to social norms, irritable and aggressive and lack of remorse.

A study of rapists and serial killers brain scans showed a lack of activity in the regions associated with empathy and remorse, and Brady was famous for his cantankerous, changeable and uncooperative nature.

Others have been diagnosed as psychotic. The difference is: Psychopathy is a personality disorder manifested in people who use a mixture of charm, manipulation, intimidation, and occasionally violence to control others, in order to satisfy their own selfish needs.

Psychotic by comparison, psychosis is when a person loses sense of reality. There is often the claim of hearing voices, or signs for them to follow.

The conditions share certain traits, but typically psychopaths are manipulative and know right from wrong, psychotics suffer from delusions.

However, all of these findings fail to reveal why other people with similar brain abnormalities, or personality traits are not serial killers.

Furthermore, the cause of this brain damage is also not known or confirmed.

There is undoubtedly a relationship between psychopathy and serial killers which is particularly interesting, it can also be seen clearly in series rapists, habitual domestic violence perpetrators as well, it may be as well to consider that both these latter groups could almost certainly easily become murderers at any given time.

All psychopaths do not become serial murderers. Rather, serial murderers may possess some, or many of the traits consistent with psychopathy.

Psychopaths who commit serial murder do not value human life and are extremely callous in their interactions with their victims.

This is evident in sexually motivated serial killers who repeatedly target, stalk, assault, and kill without any remorse. Psychopathy alone does not explain the motivations of a serial killer.

Types of serial killers:

Serial killers are typically classified in two ways, one based on motive, the other on organisational and social patterns.

Not every serial killer falls into a single type, and these classifications don't explain what leads someone to become a serial killer.

However, serial killers can be act-focused, and kill quickly, or process-focused, and kill slowly.

For act-focused killers, killing is about the act itself. Visionary murders in this group hear voices or has visions that direct him to do so, while Missionary murders believe they are meant to get rid of a particular group of people.

Alternatively, process-focused serial killers get enjoyment from torture and the death of their victims.

Lust killers derive sexual pleasure from killing.

Thrill killers get a thrill from it.

Gain killers murder because they believe they will profit in some way.

Power killers wish to be in charge of life & death.

There are always tell tale signs, that is why details, knowledge, experience and patience are the gold tool set for capturing and containing these horrendous killers.

15, 751 children and youths between 10 and 17 were cautioned or sentenced in England and Wales in 2020-2021, official figures from the Youth Justice Statistics.

London, Yorkshire and the West Midlands are still the highest youth crime areas. 3,500 proven knife and offensive weapon offences were committed by children. 8,800 first time entrants to the youth justice system. Although, these figures are horrific, for every one of those 3,500 offences there are many more than 3,500 victims, family, friends, communities are all affected.

However, this is a significant decrease figure of 19% from the previous year, this may well be attributed to the Covid pandemic and less social time or time on the streets for the children and youths, the next figures out in January 2023 for this year will be very telling.

Public Disorder, robbery, and burglary are also still high on the youngsters' offending list. There are six young offender institutions (YOIs) in England & Wales:

Cookham Wood - house up to 178 boys and young men.

Feltham - house up to 768 juveniles & young offenders

Parc - The YOI is part of a Cat B prison, all young offenders here are serving 20 years or more for the most violent crimes, latest figures 92 inmates.

Werrington - houses up to 118 detainees. Wetherby - houses up to 300 offenders.

HM Prison Bronzefield is currently one of only two prisons to house Category A prisoners in the female estate (female and juvenile category-A prisoners are called "restricted status" prisoners).

All of the above establishments take juveniles from 15 years old, from 10 - 15 perpetrators are housed in Secure Children's Homes, there are 14 throughout England and Wales.

The number of children in custody in England and Wales is expected to more than double by 2024. The National Audit Office reports that the forecast is based on the collective impact of recruiting 23,000 additional police officers, reversing COVID-19 court backlogs, and tougher sentencing following the passing of the Police, Crime, Sentencing and Courts Reform Bill.

10 years ago, in the UK we did not have any young offenders with life tariffs now we are close to the hundreds.

In total there are 70+ criminals in the British prison system that will never see the light of day again. At least not outside of a prison exercise yard.

Whole life orders are not given out lightly. To sentence someone to spend the rest of their life behind bars, you have to be pretty sure that their crimes merit the sentence and that rehabilitation is extremely unlikely.

The majority of those British criminals looking at genuine life means life sentences are in prison, because of the direction of a High Court judge after a jury trial. Among the more infamous murderers who will die in jail include:

- Grindr Killer Stephen Port
- Sian O'Callaghan and Becky Godden's killer Christopher Halliwell
- Mancunian gangster Stephen McColl

- Scottish serial killer Peter Tobin (died)
- Bullseye Killer John Cooper
- Cop killer Dale Cregan
- Peterborough ditch murderer Joanna Dennehy
- The Suffolk Strangler Steve Wright
- Lee Rigby's killer Michael Adebolajo
- The Bus Stop Stalker, serial killer & rapist Levi Bellfield
- Coventry triple killer and rapist Anthony Russell
- Reading terror attacker Khairi Saadallah

Judicially, very few people outrank trial judges. One figure who does, however, is the Home Secretary. In outstanding circumstances, The Secretary of State for the Home Department can directly impose the order themselves. It's a move usually reserved for extremely high profile and disturbing crimes.

There are currently more than 70 inmates serving entire life sentences that have been handed to them by a Home Secretary. As you may expect, it reads like a who's who of British criminal notoriety.

- Rose West
- John Childs
- Robert Maudsley
- Peter Moore
- Malcolm Green
- Mark Robinson
- Arthur Hutchinson
- Anthony Arkwright
- Victor Miller
- John Duffy
- Jeffrey Bamber among others.

Dishonourable mentions:

The following infamous British serial killers were also given whole life sentences by the Home Secretary at the time of their sentencing, but have since died:

- Dr. Death Harold Shipman
- Muswell Hill Murderer Dennis Nilsen
- Moors Murderers Ian Brady and Myra Hindley

- Child Killer Robert Black

- The Gay Slayer Colin Ireland

- Camden Ripper! Anthony Hardy

Rose West

Between 2002 and 2014, Rosemary West was the only woman in the British prison system serving a whole life order. Initially, the infamous Gloucester killer was sentenced to a minimum of 25 years for the murders of 10 young women (including her own daughter and stepdaughter), committed with her equally depraved husband Fred. Two years later, Jack Straw was installed as the new Home Secretary under Tony Blair and ordered for her to never again walk the streets.

John Childs

East End gangster and hitman Childs was Britain's most sought-after, effective and elusive contract killer of the 1970s. Eventually apprehended at the end of the decade, he admitted to having carried out six murders for money, although no bodies or remains were ever discovered. He later confessed to a further five murders while inside. He implicated two other criminals in his crimes, both of whom were convicted.

It was later found that Childs had perjured himself in the process and the men were innocent. After that, the pathological liar was given his order never to leave prison.

Robert Maudsley

Britain's longest-serving prisoner is known for being dangerous. In fact, his reputation as an inmate is perhaps second only to a certain **Charlie Bronson.** It's warranted too. At least it used to be anyway. After all, you don't get the nickname Hannibal the Cannibal for nothing, do you? Maudsley was sent to Broadmoor in 1973 after strangling a man called John Farrell. Since then, he's killed three more men, all while inside. The nickname comes from the special cell he's kept in. Well, that and because he ate some of one victim's brain. It's no huge surprise that Robert Maudsley won't ever be allowed out of prison.

Peter Moore

Despite challenging the order with the European Court of Human Rights, Peter The Man in Black, Moore couldn't get his whole life order overturned., he'll die in prison after he was handed down the harshest sentence it's possible to receive in the UK.

His crimes? Moore was a sadistic serial killer who

killed and mutilated four men in Wales in 1995. He was also found guilty of a further 40 serious sexual assaults and rapes of men over a 20-year period. Moore was friends inside with Dr Harold Shipman until Shipman's suicide in 2004.

Malcolm Green

In late 1989, Malcolm Green attacked, killed and dismembered a tourist from New Zealand. It was a particularly callous murder as he then wrapped the various body parts and scattered them far and wide across South Wales. The murder earned him a whole life order. Why? Well, it had to be taken into account that Green had previously served an 18 year stretch for killing a sex worker. It was decided that he would likely kill again were he to be released at any point.

Mark Robinson

Mark Robinson, like several others on this list, first received a life sentence for a murder he committed. After two and a half decades, Robinson would be eligible for parole. Like Malcolm Green, Robinson's last conviction really would be his last after an earlier murder conviction was taken into account and a whole life tariff was imposed from on high. Understandably so.

Arthur Hutchinson

In 1984, then Home Secretary Leon Brittan handed down a whole life order to the rapist and spree killer Arthur Hutchinson. Despite multiple appeals, the sentence is always upheld. It seems that no one is prepared to let the Hartlepool-born monster be released on their watch. He'll almost certainly die in prison.

Anthony Arkwright

At just 21, Anthony Arkwright is the youngest person in Britain to receive a life means life sentence. In 1988, across two days, he beat and hacked up three people, including his own grandfather.

Victor Miller

A sadist and prolific rapist of young boys, Victor Miller finally tipped the balance and killed a 14- year-old boy from Worcestershire in 1988. He was, like many other killers here, initially dished out a 25-year life sentence. Unusually, he requested a whole life order, asking to die in prison and never be released. The Home Secretary at the time, Douglas Hurd, agreed.

John Duffy

The Railway Killer and rapist John Duffy was found

guilty of killing two women and raping seven more in the late eighties. The true numbers were no doubt higher. He received a 30-year sentence for his sickening crimes and would have been considered for parole in 2018 were he not later been handed a whole life order. One of the reasons was that he worked with an accomplice who he refused to name.

Jeffrey Bamber

The White House Farm murderer Jeffrey Bamber was found guilty of slaughtering his adoptive parents, his sister and his young twin nephews. He carried out the atrocity at the family's remote Essex farmhouse in August 1985. 14 months later he was convicted. Bamber's trial judge sentenced him to 25 years, but admitted that it seemed very unlikely that he would ever be released. Subsequent Home Secretaries tend to agree.

Through the decades of official studies on serial killers, they focus entirely on themselves and the power they are able to assert over others. It has also shown that through years of profiling serial killers, key traits that many have in common.

- Adult antisocial behaviour

- Early behavioural problems

- Lack of responsibility
- Need for excitement
- Poor behaviour controls
- Impulsive
- Shallow emotions
- Deceitful and manipulative
- Lack of empathy
- Lack of remorse or guilt
- Egocentric and grandiose
- Smooth talking but insincere

These individuals over time, all or most of these traits come to light in each of their histories, their behaviour and their lack of remorse.

All serial killers have mothers, fathers, some have siblings and extended family, some have spouses, even fewer have children; there are also associates in crime and a few acquaintances, as there are not so many friends.

Do they ever think of the consequences for their circle?

In all honesty, probably the answer is no. Being part of their lack of empathy, self-gratification it probably never enters their thoughts at the time of offending and after conviction, they will expect them to get on with it.

All serial murders are not sexually based. There are many other motivations for serial murders including anger, thrill, financial gain, and attention seeking.

• Anger is a powerful motivation in which the offender displays rage or hostility toward either a certain subgroup of the population such as the homeless, or society as a whole.

• Attention seeking, due to massive media exposure, certain serial killers such as Myra Hindley & Ian Brady become what I call "celebrity monsters" in our popular culture. However, the media are not alone in creating celebrity monsters. Some serial killers actually seek out public notoriety and actively engage in the creation of their public image.

• Financial gain is a motivation in which the offender benefits monetarily from killing that is not drug, gang or organised crime related. A few examples of these types of crimes are comfort/gain killings, robbery- homicide, or multiple killings involving insurance or welfare fraud.

- Ideology is a motivation to commit murder in order to further the goals and ideas of a specific individual or group. Examples of these include terrorist groups, or an individual(s) who attacks a specific racial, gender, or ethnic group out of sheer hatred for the particular group.

- Power/thrill is a motivation in which the offender feels empowered and/or exhilarated when he kills his victims. The act of killing is an end in itself.

- Psychosis is a rare situation in which the offender is suffering from a severe mental illness and is killing specifically because of that illness. The condition may include auditory and/or visual hallucinations and paranoid, grandiose or bizarre delusions.

- Sexually based is a motivation driven by the sexual needs or desires of the offender. There may or may not be evidence of sexual contact present at the crime scene.

However, there are many other facets to consider with serial killers:

- The motive can be very difficult to determine in a serial murder investigation.

- A serial murderer can have multiple motives for committing his/her crimes.

- A serial killer's motive(s) can evolve both within a single murder and throughout the series of murders.

- The classification of motivations should be limited to observable behaviour and conditions at the scenes of the murders.

- Even if a motive can be identified, it may not be helpful in identifying a serial murderer.

- Utilising investigative resources to discern the motive instead of identifying the offender can derail or bog down an investigation.

- Investigators should not necessarily equate a serial murderer's motivation(s) with the level of injury.

Finally, regardless of the specific motive(s), most serial killers commit their crimes because they want to. The exception to this would be those few serial killers suffering from a severe mental illness for whom no coherent motive exists.

Serial Killer Genes = MAOA & CDH13?

Monoamine oxidase A (MAOA) has often been labelled the "warrior gene" for its association with higher levels of aggression in response to provocation. According to certain studies, individuals with low levels of the gene are more likely to respond aggressively when they think they have been wrong, which is a gene linked to high levels of aggression in its low-activity form.

CDH13 also contributes to maintaining excitatory and inhibitory functions. It has been suggested that disturbed neural connectivity is the main pathophysiological mechanism underlying behavioural problems in attention deficit hyperactivity disorder (ADHD), a disorder whose core symptom is losing impulse control. Thus, it is strongly associated with violent criminality.

It's estimated that about one-third of the population of Western civilisation carries the low- activity form of the MAOA gene, however the population that are serial killers is far less than 1%.

Not Just Genes Alone

Common traits in serial killers include sensation seeking, a lack of remorse or guilt, impulsivity, a need for control, and predatory behaviour. All of these character traits are consistent with psychopathic personality disorder.

Many studies have suggested, there is a myriad of environmental factors that can play a pivotal role in the formation of a homicidal mind. Some factors that have been suggested are an estranged father, low socioeconomic status, lack of maternal sensitivity, poor living conditions, childhood abuse, and many others. However, there are serial killers that do not come from these backgrounds and there are multitudes of people that come from similar backgrounds that do not go on to become serial killers.

The question remains: Are serial killers born with a desire to kill, or is it something that they develop over the course of their lives? Nurture or nature. Well, it seems that both genetics and conditioning may play a role in the creation of a serial murderer.

The conditions that result in a serial killer are complex and varied.

True Crime People & Places

True Crime People & Places

Part 6

Serial Killer Articles:

The English term and concept of serial killer are commonly attributed to former FBI Special agent Robert Ressler, who used the term serial homicide in 1974 in a lecture at Police Staff Academy in Bramshill, Hampshire, England.

Over the centuries, there have been hundreds of documented cases of serial murder around the world, but the term serial killer is relatively new.

Today, however, serial murder, also called serial killing, the unlawful homicide of at least two people carried out by the same person (or persons) in separate events occurring at different times. Although, this definition is widely accepted, the crime is not formally recognised in any legal code.

However, when we look a little deeper, the term serial killer comes to light a lot earlier:

It has been said that the term Serial Killer was first used by a writer Dorothy B. Hughes in her A Lonely

Place book published in1947.

I have looked but can't actually find the term, but there are a lot of murders in a series.

In 1950 the term serial murder was used in The Complete Detective; being the life and strange and exciting cases of Raymond Schindler, master detective by Richard Hughes.

Historian Robert Eisler, used the term serial killings in a lecture he gave in 1948 at the Royal Society of Medicine in London. Though it was in reference to the continual killings by Punch and Judy, so does not really fit the criteria.

Taking the words internationally there are many more examples of the exact term, used with the present day meaning.

One such contender is Ernest August Ferdinand Gennat, a famous German detective from Berlin. He revolutionised police work with the process we now call profiling and he set up the first murder squad.

The infamous serial killers Peter Kurten and Fritz Haarmann were also part of his work history, in 1930 he used the term Serien-morder, which directly translates to serial murder, then easily to serial killer.

In Germany in the 1920s and 1930s there were

several high profile serial killing cases, just as there were in the 1970s and 1980s in the USA, so Gennat bought the concept of serial killers to light in the 30s as Ressler did in the 70s.

There is one other to quote, but unfortunately the Dutch journalist is unknown, wrote a review of the film Come of Amos in 1925 for the Algemeen Handelsblad newspaper mentioning a serie-moordenaar in an article.

So that may be the first one?

Serial Killers are Different

Less than 1% of our population are serial killers - Thank goodness!

There are grades of perpetrators and likewise grades or categories of prisons. They vary in their security, staffing levels, housing (i.e. single or double cell occupancy), wing placement.

The A to D category listing is deemed on three points:

Risk of escape

Harm to the public, if they were to escape

Threat to the control and stability of a prison

The lower the threat of the prisoner the lower the category of prison they will be housed in. Category A being the highest to category D being the lowest.

This is for adult male inmates, women, youths 15

- 21, children 10 - 15 are defined differently.

Category A These are high security prisons. They house male prisoners who, if they were to escape, pose the most threat to the public, the police, or national security.

Category B These prisons are either local or training prisons.

Local prisons house prisoners that are taken directly from court in the local area (sentenced or on remand), and training prisons hold long-term and high-security prisoners.

Category C These prisons are training and resettlement prisons; most prisoners are located in a category C. They provide prisoners with the opportunity to develop their own skills so they can find work and resettle back into the community on release.

Category D - open prisons These prisons have

minimal security and allow eligible prisoners to spend most of their day away from the prison on licence to carry out work, education or for other resettlement purposes. Open prisons only house prisoners that have been risk-assessed and deemed suitable for open conditions.

There are currently 122 prisons in England and Wales, 32 are the original Victorian fortresses.

12 are women's prisons, 5 are Young Offenders Institutions, there are 8 category A prisons for men, 2 category A prisons for women. In England and Wales the current prison population is around 88,205.

1,028 are classified as cat A prisoners and 72 of the cat A prisoners have full life tariffs.

Although we are seeing a huge influx of crime programmes, a monumental increase of interest in serial killers, most of which stems from the media and entertainment industry. In reality, serial killers are a tiny percentage of our everyday crime, murder, manslaughter and rape unfortunately are much more likely to affect the general public.

Serial Killing Near You

Glasgow, Manchester and Yorkshire have produced more serial killers than any other areas.

Archibald Hall, Ian Brady, Colin Norris,, Anthony Arkwright, John Christie, Peter Sutcliffe

Part 7

FAQs for Linda:

People often ask me - Do you remember your first time going into a prison?

Most definitely, my first prison was HMP Canterbury, the lofty towers and the majestic front door and archway, made me hold my breath, just for a while.

I was excited and nervous all at the same time, I was there to see a prisoner, a young man that I had been working with via the Medway probation office. He had reoffended and was sent on remand to Canterbury, on the charge of killing his girlfriend's baby.

The security searches then were not as vigorous as today, but the clunk of the metal doors and the grind of the well worn keys in the old locks has never changed. I was with a lawyer, a young intern gathering information and details for a higher legal mind. We passed through quite easily and prisoners on remand have a little more freedom than their convicted inmates.

Then he could have cigarettes and chocolate while we were with him and messages from his family, not something that goes on today.

I was in this small stifling room for 90 mins and I remember feeling like I had been down drains when I came out, all I wished for on the drive home was a bath and change of clothes.

My full time work in prisons did not come for a long time after this, but I did do other visits of prisoners in that time.

My full time in prisons came through a friend, she was based at HMP Maidstone then a Cat B prison, they were short staffed and asked me if I would like to help out. I agreed and as we say the rest is history.

Maidstone was a similar structure to Canterbury, both Victorian built prisons with many of the same issues internally and maintenance wise. Listed

buildings are a nightmare, their age, constant use and misuse take their toll it is a never ending bill keeping them up to standard.

Cookham Wood a female prison in Rochester was home to Myra Hindley and Maidstone among many others the Krays. However, the true feeling of foreboding did not come until I went into Holloway the very famous London female prison, which was also a hanging prison, it was closed in 2016. Once the largest women's prison in Western Europe. Over its 164 year history, Holloway Prison saw the force-feeding of suffragettes on hunger strike, to the UK's last execution of a woman, Ruth Ellis in 1955.

Thousands of women passed through its gates, each with their own unique story.

The Scrubs (Wormwood Scrubs), a really imposing and possibly the most photographed front door in crime films and series, it holds an equally gruesome history as Holloway, but for men.

Originally built between 1875 and 1891 by convict labour, it has been home to most of the most heinous inmates, Ian Brady, Dennis Nilsen, Charles Bronson to name a few.

When working within mental health it is crucial to have solid boundaries, for ourself, or we can suffer a lot. I found that I felt safer and more secure dealing with the perpetrators than I did with the victims.

Once again, my pathway opened up for me as I walked along it, the teaching and training came a lot later, even more so the writing, but I had been encouraged by many throughout the decades to write, I just never thought about it seriously until

after the people closest to me my mum, dad and husband had died. Funny how people see things in us, that we don't see for ourselves, until we want to.

People often ask me "What it is like sitting face to face with killers, sex offenders, and psychopaths?"

If only people could grow horns and a tail, it would make detection so much easier, or in the old cowboy movies where a baddy wore a black hat and a goody wore a white hat and always got his girl, but reality is not like that, or even that simple.

The reality of working in a prison is that life is not 'normal' it is very regimented, organised and logistics are key to safety. Knowing where every person is and accountable for. You have to be mentally aware and be respect the environment, something simple can easily be turned into a weapon, a hostage situation can easily occur just by being dismissive of the system or cutting corners.

The truth is I am probably more vulnerable and at risk standing at a bus stop than I ever was in any of the foreboding fortresses that we have as some of our prisons.

We have no idea who that stranger is that speaks to us, seemly passing the time of day and a few pleasantries. Whereas on the wings and in the corridors of any A or B category prison, I already know who and what these people are and what they are capable of.

Some get notorious names such as Myra Hindley, Ian Brady, Ronnie & Reggie Kray, Rose West etc., but they are the tiny tip of the ice burg. There are thousands of horrific killers, rapists and violent criminals who are now housed in our prison system.

Externally they look just like you and me, the difference what goes on internally. I am not including the ravages of long term drug or alcohol misuse which many of the prison population are affected by, but methodical criminals are generally not addicts, because the level of planning, the logistics and continued predatory nature means they are lucid.

Addicts usually are the more opportunistic criminals, feeding their habit is their prime importance. It can be said that some serial killers are addicted to their crimes, and as they get more confident the desires become more demanding, but that is a different type of an addiction to the repetitive demand of drugs and alcohol.

Walking out of the prison at the end of the day

means leaving these people behind, keeping a balance between personal and professional is a challenge. Going home and leaving the conversations and images is hard, because you cannot bring it through the front door into over dinner conversation.

My car was always my pressure valve, many tears, shouts, and solitude have been part of my journey home, sometimes even sat in the prison car park, or in a supermarket car park, in the privacy and safety of my own zone. Letting go is essential, I have seen many colleagues find support in alcohol, drugs, gambling and affairs, which all take their toll. My vice was eating, I gained a lot of weight, the last thing I wanted to feel was attractive, it made me vulnerable.

I know that I take life behind bars fairly for granted, it is not glamorous, nor is it horrific, human beings find ways to adapt to surroundings and a different type of life develops, a society, a pecking order is defined, rules, friendships and education are all part of their daily life.

People often ask me. Do you feel afraid inside a prison?"

It is an unusual and unnatural world, where many varied individuals are thrown together in an insular environment. In England and Wales 32 of the 122 prisons are the imposing Victorian fortresses, with huge stone walls ensconced with swirls of barbed and razor wire on top of them.

Drab-looking buildings with small non-glass windows covered with sturdy metal grills. There is also a continual defense of fortified, large mental gates, breaking each section of a prison off from the other.

Going into a prison via the workers/visitors' gate is a very different experience from entering as an inmate, fortunately, I can only talk about that from an onlooker's perspective.

Clearly, security is a given, no mobile phones or gadgets are permitted into a prison, photo ID, badges, fingerprints, sniffer dogs, bag searches, and frisking to access even the first set of doors, before getting out any set of keys. The keys are usually housed in electronic cabinets with fingerprint access, which is all great until it is a cold day and my fingertip shrivels, or a hot day when it is all clammy. I often struggled at this stage and annoyingly kept others waiting because my finger would not register.

We all have substantial key belts and pouches with a chain to attach the set of allocated keys. To access a radio, the whole finger exercise was repeated, so getting into and out of work in itself can be a long process daily. I did not often go out for lunch!

In most communal rooms, i.e., education, workshops, and meeting rooms there is also an emergency button which is connected to the central command centre in each prison. In some of the extended buildings, like portacabins, there was also a phone.

Walking onto, or through the wings, I must say that I have never felt threatened, mostly the residents just like a passing hello or acknowledgement, apart from anyone specific I was going to speak to. I must admit that prison does have certain smells, atmospheres and noises that we come accustomed to, being away from them is when you notice it.

In the classrooms or meeting rooms, there are no officers present, except to bring them to the room, come in at break time to accompany people to the bathroom, and take them back to their wing at the end of a session, I was not permitted to escort any prisoner on my own from one location to another. Logistics is a key factor in moving around the prison and the central command centre runs that.

Talking to prisoners, they like us all have good days and bad days, if they have an appeal, or a court date, a visit or a letter all sorts of emotions can bubble and boil which in turn will affect how they interacted with me. Access to medical, dentist and opticians are difficult, so even a toothache can alter a person's willingness to engage.

Yes, I have witnessed/broken up fights, tantrums, and individuals collapsing with drugs, especially spice. Everyone who works in a frontline environment faces verbal abuse and threats, they are part of a day's

work. However, fearing for my own life, I have never been in such a situation. There are more attacks on prison guards than on other staff members.

Luckily, I have never been in prison when a riot has been active, however, I have seen images of the aftermath and that is scary to imagine how violent and disengaged the rioters must have been.

There are basics, of course, keep my personal details - personal, we all make up stories about where we live, what we drive, if we have kids/husbands etc. Intelligence is a currency in prison and they will take time to piece things together and if they can manipulate or threaten with them if an opportunity arises they will. All prisoners in my experience are sorry, - sorry they got caught, because if they hadn't, they would have carried on doing it. There are remorseful inmates, but there are also many who are not. They will test the waters of corruption jokingly; they may even initiate a discussion about coercion to see if there is any leeway. I always, stopped them in the first instance and just said if this conversation continues, I will report it. When they know where they stand with you, from my experience they will accept that. If they think there is room for manipulation, they will jump on that too. However, there is a place for a laugh, joke and banter, as long as you are aware of any undertones.

I often say when I am inside a prison, I know the people I am with, who they are and what they are capable of, I am more vulnerable in a bus queue or in a busy shopping centre, because who knows who is there and with what intention.

I must admit each time I came out of a prison and that last gate thudded shut behind me, I was thankful to be back in the real world, I still choose to sit with my back to a wall in any public space and count the number of people in a room. I guess some things are so ingrained that they will not change even on the outside.

People often ask me: Who is the worst person you have spoken to?"

This is hard question mainly because for me each

person I speak to is the worst person at the time, every person has harmed, or killed somebody, has negatively affected the lives of others and caused untold heartache and pain, not just for their victims, but for all their family, friends and their communities.

It is easy to put defensive barriers up when going into a room with somebody, or a group, but that would be exhausting. It is hard to explain, but I got to feel comfortable in my surroundings, even if I was changing prisons, there is a normality in their rigid regimes, a safety in knowing the process. Most definitely time, experience and age help, but in my experience, engagement is the important element.

Many would walk in with hostile attitudes, defiant, wanting to shout the odds about their innocence, how it was everyone else's fault, the system was corrupt, but once the letting off of steam was done, mostly I would then be able to have civil and many enlightening conversations. These were more likely to be the more violent, aggressive, often re offending individuals. Others come in quiet, no eye contact, these are often first time offenders, possibly in for manslaughter, in a fight or motor accident, or prisoners that had already served some of their sentence and had settled into the routine.

Many of the life/long term prisoners are calmer once

they have accepted their sentence, I never had an issue with most of them. Some could be rude, curt and petulant, unless they wanted something, then the charm offensive would be there. Of course, prisoners like us all have good days and bad days and there is a lot of frustration in prison, lack of control in particular. Also, if there are issues within their family or relationships, it could be just as simple as not getting a piece of bread with their lunch, that could put all of their emotions out of kilt.

Getting over this and getting to know them as a person and not as their crimes is the only way to work.

There are dangerous people inside and outside of prison, they can be close to you, or strangers, this is an issue none of the individuals I have worked with

have grown horns and a tail, they are just human beings, externally they look just like you and me, the deviance and malevolence is just below the surface.

"Why did you choose prisons?"

Let me say, it was never my childhood dream to spend my adult life in and out of prisons.

We are going back many decades now to when I was looking at leaving school and making a choice of career. To be honest, I did not have a clue, I was very tempted to the police, but remember women in those days were not thought of and were certainly not equals in the force as it was then.

The only thing in my life my father ever refused me with no discussion was to sign an application form for the WRAF. So, that was a no go.

I was the first in our family to go to university and my dad was so proud, he had visions of a doctor or solicitor in the family. When I went off to Canterbury (Kent) University Open Day, I had no idea what I was going to be looking for, I was just excited about going. I had my own little light blue Ford Escort and I felt very grown up, going on this adventure.

I was impressed with the buildings and structure of the university, so many people there, people chattering, and the Dons in what seemed like regal robes.

I spoke to several people, but even as an eager as I was they did not light a spark, until, I spoke with one man and he had listened to me intently then said I should go and listen to a lecture, which I did. The lecture was about psychology and the fascinating world of what goes on inside our brain. I was hooked.

Much to my dad's dismay I made a choice, he was

far from impressed, until several decades later when I did my Honours Degree in Education, did he think that was a proper qualification. However, I have been so amazingly lucky, I do not feel that I have worked many days in my whole life. Each day is different and often a challenge, but also enlightening.

While studying I struggled a bit with Humanistic, and Psychodynamic fields of Rogers and Freud, they always seemed a little "fluffy" to me, so easy for manipulation and mostly long term treatment plans. When I first came across Ulric Neisser and Albert Ellis the spark was fanned and cognitive/REBT psychology was where I was headed.

I think I have been very fortunate in my time, when I started, psychology was not a household word, mental health was lock them up and throw away the key, counselling and behavioural therapy did not exist for the general population and criminal profiling was not taken seriously until 1986 when Dr. David Canter successfully profiled the Railway Rapist, but still many policing areas were skeptical.

I have seen many changes, more openness about mental health, more understanding of cognitive function, more research on all areas of brain, genes and emotional development. We know more, but we certainly don't know all - yet.

I did not start in the prisons until later, in fact probation and victim support for my first areas of practice, Kent police have always been a forward thinking constabulary and through people I had met while studying, doors opened and opportunities arose. That leads to another question for another day.

People often ask me: How do you leave the heinous, violent criminal behind when you come home?

Many people have the same issue, not only violent criminals, but their work in general. Professions that work with particularly traumatic environments do need to take care of their mental and physical wellbeing. However, like for most of us I found out the hard way too.

I would say particularly front line careers and anyone in a caring profession usually gives to others more than to themselves, even to the extreme point of putting off going to the toilet, finishing something for somebody else. I was no different. Long hours, I can cope attitude took me to the dark pits of burnout in 2005.

Juggling a demanding career, caring for two infirm, elderly parents, fighting the educational system for my hyperactive child on the autistic spectrum and living with her took their toll. I left the prisons and entered training and teaching, a much more peaceful routine for me to have time to heal myself.

It is hard to be in any high pressured workplace and walk through the front door smiling, what shall we have for tea tonight? Leaving the ugliness at the front gate. For many of my colleagues alcohol, drugs, sexual affairs often are used for support to blot out some of the awful things we see and hear, I was lucky my emotional support was food. It added many inches to my hips, but it was certainly much easier to take back the control of my life than batting the other addictions.

Like many confidential professions we cannot come home and talk about what we did that day, that is why having a professional to offload to is essential, with all the cut backs supervision was always reduced and minimalised, but it is worth the investment in ourselves and I was very fortunate to have good support most of the time, I had to provide my own at various stages, but even now I have people I talk to and of course my journals, writing has always been part of my life, but just for me, it has taken me a very long, probably too long to use this medium to better potential.

As I have mentioned before, choosing what is right for you and keeping your boundaries is essential.

Gratitude and positivity are my pillars, I can't say I have every been very religious, but I do believe in God, I would say I am probably more spiritual, calmness and quiet are my sanctuary whether indoors, in a church or a swimming pool.

Learning to compartmentalise is also a trait of front line professions, this can be difficult at first, but it is also difficult when we get really good at it, because it is easy to become detached, isolated and aloof. Most frontline professions have a dark humour and yes, to a certain amount we get accustomed to levels of violence, it is important to keep a reality check.

I have always had good close friends, a small number that last many decades in some cases. Some great mentors and wonderful opportunities. Looking back, I feel very privileged and happy to have been able to be a small cog in a part of criminal justice history.

How do you face infamous criminals inside a prison?

It is true that some criminals seem to get selected by the press for one reason or another & then the local, national or even global interest starts and develops.

Serial killers of course are continually news worthy even when they are dead, Jack the Ripper proves this point, beyond any doubt. Some have quirks or play to the media, others may be physically attractive, but their lives and choices are intriguing.

You often see in series and films about the amount of fan mail some prisoners receive, this is not fictitious, there are many people who want to get to know them more, many want to know them intimately, there have been several high profile marriages behind bars, Reggie Kray in Maidstone, Charles Bronson twice in Wakefield, Julian Assange in Belmarsh.

These people do achieve a type of celebrity. status and in prison there is most definitely a hierarchy, but there is also somebody who thinks they can take them down a notch or two. Like all people in the limelight, some handle it well, some don't, some like to play on it, just like society they have different personalities.

Sitting in a room with them, as I have mentioned before is not hard, because they are in captivity, but most certainly and rightly there are protocols and security systems in place, for everyone's protection. Without a doubt when violent criminals are free, they are in our world, with the various expectations of society, but when we are in prison, it is their world, we as staff may manage it, but with their co-operation.

Prisoners see staff as a resource, their day consists of what can you do for me? Prisoners will ask seemingly innocent questions, then put their heads together to outline and profile the staff member, especially if they are new, where they live, what their house is like, what family they have, what car they drive, there is a world of information in these answers. The underlying test here is - are they corruptible or bribable.

There is a very fine line not to cross when working in prisons, privacy and transparency, the moment there are any secrets, life becomes very difficult, I have seen many good professionals lose jobs and even sit on the other side of the bars through manipulation.

In all of the years I years I have been in and out of many prisons, there have been many changes, it is a tough environment, but I would not change it. There have been some amazing characters, there have been some very sad people, there have been a lot of arrogant people, much of that being bravado in a difficult and unnatural place. Accepting their sentence, especially the long terms, is a huge step for them. They can start to make a new type of life then, instead of constantly comparing to their previous life.

However, in answer to the question, How do I Face infamous criminals inside a prison? Very simple as a person, whether one at a time or in groups. Our first meeting is always the most important, they don't know me, or trust me, they have probably seen other professionals come and go. Set the boundaries, make no promises I can't keep and keep them informed, like us all not knowing and waiting for answers is frustrating, that would then work against me on further meetings. All humans like to be listened to.

Unravelling the Psychological Parallels: Ghislaine Maxwell and Myra Hindley

As a dedicated student of human behaviour and psychology, I find immense value in examining the psychological traits and patterns that emerge in high-profile criminal cases. Today, we embark on a thought-provoking exploration of the intriguing psychological similarities between Ghislaine Maxwell and Myra Hindley. Though their respective cases differ greatly, delving into their psyche can offer valuable insights into the complexities of human behaviour.

Ghislaine Maxwell: The Enabler

Ghislaine Maxwell, formerly associated with the notorious Jeffrey Epstein, faced numerous charges related to her involvement in enabling Epstein's exploitation of young girls. Maxwell's case highlights a critical psychological characteristic: the role of an enabler. Enablers often exhibit traits such as manipulation, coercion, and an insatiable thirst for power and control. They exert influence over others, actively participating in the maintenance of a toxic environment while facilitating criminal activities.

Myra Hindley: The Manipulator

Myra Hindley, infamous for her involvement in the chilling Moors Murders, offers a distinct psychological profile. Hindley's role centered around manipulation, skillfully using her charm and charisma to entice young people to Ian Brady. Without a doubt, she also participated in committing heinous crimes against children.

Manipulators like Hindley possess the ability to influence and persuade others, capitalising on vulnerabilities for their personal gain.

Common Psychological Traits

Despite the unique circumstances of their cases, Ghislaine Maxwell and Myra Hindley share several psychological traits that serve as common denominators. These include: Narcissism: Both individuals displayed self- centredness, a need for admiration, and a shocking lack of empathy towards their victims. Their actions revolved solely around personal gratification, with no regard for the suffering they inflicted.

Power and Control: Maxwell and Hindley wielded control over others, leveraging their influence to dominate and manipulate those within their sphere of influence. The desire for power and the need to maintain control fuelled their criminal pursuits.

Deviant Sexual Behaviour: The involvement of Maxwell and Hindley in sexual exploitation and deviant acts sheds light on a darker aspect of their personalities. Their willingness to engage in such activities demonstrates a disturbing disregard for the well-being of others.

Emotional Manipulation: Both individuals were masters at exploiting others' emotions and vulnerabilities to further their own agendas. Their ability to manipulate and coerce others played a pivotal role in their criminal endeavours.

Lessons Learned

Studying individuals like Ghislaine Maxwell and Myra Hindley extends beyond mere curiosity. It offers profound lessons and valuable insights into the intricate web of human behaviour. By understanding the psychological traits and patterns exhibited by these individuals, we equip ourselves to recognise the signs of manipulation, control, and exploitation. Both women were in toxic relationships with partners who undeniably had serious heinous psychological traits and they were both enthralled by them. Such knowledge becomes a powerful tool in preventing future crimes and fostering a safer society for all.

Conclusion

The psychological similarities between Ghislaine Maxwell and Myra Hindley shed light on the intricacies of human behaviour and the disturbing capabilities some individuals possess.

Recognising the traits of enablers and manipulators, such as narcissism, a thirst for power, deviant sexual behaviour, and emotional manipulation, allows us to be more vigilant in our communities. By engaging in open and constructive discussions, we can work together to prevent such crimes and foster an environment of safety, empathy, and understanding for all.

Part 8

Coercive Control & Stalking

Recognising the Severe Impacts of Non-Fatal Strangulation: A Milestone for Domestic Abuse Legislation

On June 7, 2022, England and Wales took a significant step forward in addressing domestic abuse by introducing the offence of non-fatal strangulation and suffocation. This ground breaking development highlights the growing recognition of strangulation as a particularly dangerous aspect of domestic violence, often intertwined with controlling and coercive behaviours.

The neuropsychological consequences of non- fatal strangulation have been extensively studied, revealing a range of serious impacts on survivors, including both physical and psychological outcomes. In this article, we delve into the alarming neurological, psychological, and cognitive changes that can result from such acts of violence.

Neuropsychological Outcomes:

Studies exploring the neuropsychological consequences of non-fatal strangulation have revealed distressing findings. The deprivation of oxygen to the brain during these traumatic incidents can result in hypoxic brain injury and even a stroke. Survivors may experience neurological outcomes such as seizures, speech disorders, paralysis, changes to vision, voice, and sensory loss. These physical consequences further underline the gravity of the act and highlight the urgent need for preventive measures and appropriate legal responses.

Psychological Outcomes:

Non-fatal strangulation has been linked to a host of severe psychological outcomes for survivors. Post-Traumatic Stress Disorder (PTSD), depression, suicidal, and dissociation are among the most prevalent consequences. The traumatic nature of the experience can have long-lasting effects on a survivor's mental well-being, often requiring professional support and therapeutic interventions. Recognising these psychological impacts is crucial for developing comprehensive support systems and tailored interventions for survivors of domestic abuse.

Cognitive and Behavioural Changes:

In addition to the physical and psychological consequences, non-fatal strangulation can lead to profound cognitive and behavioural changes. Survivors may experience memory loss, executive difficulties (such as problem-solving and judgment), and an increased tendency towards compliance with the abuser's demands.

These cognitive impairments can have a profound impact on a survivor's ability to regain control over their lives and seek help. Raising awareness about these changes is vital for both legal professionals and support services to understand the unique challenges faced by survivors and provide appropriate assistance.

The introduction of the offence of non-fatal strangulation and suffocation in England and Wales represents a crucial step in addressing domestic abuse. By recognising the gravity of this specific form of violence, the legislation acknowledges the severe neuropsychological outcomes survivors may endure. From hypoxic brain injury to PTSD and cognitive impairments, the impacts are far-reaching and demand comprehensive responses. It is imperative that society as a whole, including legal systems, healthcare providers, and support services, work collaboratively to raise awareness, provide support and prevent the occurrence of such acts. Together, we can create a safer and more compassionate environment for survivors of domestic abuse, empowering them to rebuild their lives and heal from the trauma they have endured.

Unmasking the Shadows: Exploring Different Types of Stalking

Stalking is a serious and invasive behaviour that affects countless individuals around the world. It involves persistent and unwanted attention, which can lead to psychological and emotional distress for the victim. Stalking is not limited to a single form; rather, it manifests in various ways. In this article, we will shed light on different types of stalking, highlighting their characteristics and the impact they have on victims.

Cyberstalking

With the rise of technology, a new form of stalking has emerged: cyberstalking. It involves the use of electronic communication platforms, such as social media, email, or messaging apps, to harass and intimidate the victim. Cyberstalkers may engage in activities such as sending threatening messages, spreading false information, monitoring the victim's online activities, or even hacking into their accounts.

The digital nature of this type of stalking makes it easier for perpetrators to remain anonymous and increases the sense of vulnerability for the victim.

Intimate Partner Stalking

Intimate partner stalking occurs within the context of a romantic or former romantic relationship. It involves a pattern of unwanted behaviours aimed at monitoring, controlling, or instilling fear in the victim. The stalker may follow the victim, monitor their activities, make unwanted contact, or use other means to exert power and control. Intimate partner stalking poses a significant threat to the victim's safety and often occurs alongside other forms of domestic violence and coercive controlling behaviour.

Celebrity Stalking

Celebrity stalking is a unique form of stalking that primarily targets individuals in the public eye, such as actors, musicians, or public figures. The stalker may develop an obsessive infatuation with the celebrity, leading them to engage in persistent and intrusive behaviour. This can include physical stalking, attempting to make contact, sending excessive letters or gifts, or even resorting to threats and violence. Celebrity stalking not only poses a risk to the safety and well-being of the targeted individual but also disrupts their personal and professional life.

Workplace Stalking

Workplace stalking occurs when a stalker focuses their attention on a colleague, superior, or subordinate in a professional setting. It involves persistent behaviours that invade the victim's privacy, such as unwanted phone calls, emails, or gifts, following the victim to and from work, or spreading rumours and false information about them. Workplace stalking can create a hostile and unsafe environment, leading to emotional distress and impairing the victim's job performance.

Stranger Stalking

Stranger stalking refers to instances where the stalker has no prior relationship or connection to the victim. The motivation for this type of stalking can vary, ranging from obsession, sexual gratification, or a desire to exert control over another person. Stranger stalkers may engage in activities such as following the victim, making unsolicited advances, leaving unwanted gifts or notes, or monitoring the victim's daily activities.

The unpredictability of stranger stalking can leave the

victim feeling vulnerable and constantly on edge.

Stalking is a pervasive issue that can have severe psychological, emotional, and physical consequences for victims. By understanding the different types of stalking, we can raise awareness, provide support to those affected, and work towards developing effective prevention and intervention strategies. It is crucial to recognise stalking behaviour early on and take appropriate action to protect the well- being and safety of individuals targeted by stalkers. Together, we can create a society where no one lives in fear of being watched and pursued against their will.

Unveiling the Shadows: Shedding Light on Domestic Abuse

Domestic abuse is a sinister force that thrives in the shadows, silently wreaking havoc on the lives of countless individuals. It transforms what should be havens of love and security into landscapes of pain, fear, and anxiety. This pervasive issue is often concealed from public view, trapping victims in a cycle of suffering. The 2019-20 Crime Survey for England and Wales (CSEW) sheds light on the alarming scope of this problem, estimating that 2.3 million people experienced domestic abuse in the preceding year.

The Silent Struggle: At the heart of all domestic abuse lies a tragic transformation of intimate relationships into breeding grounds for anguish. Victims and survivors, entangled in these toxic dynamics, face the challenge of navigating a reality that contradicts the very essence of what a home should be. The silent struggle they endure often goes unnoticed, concealed behind closed doors.

The Statistics Speak Volumes: The CSEW figures underscore the magnitude of the issue, emphasising that domestic abuse is not an isolated problem but a widespread societal concern. As we grapple with the enormity of 2.3 million people impacted in just one year, it becomes evident that this is an epidemic that demands our attention and collective action.

Breaking the Silence: One of the greatest barriers to addressing domestic abuse is the shroud of silence that envelops it. Victims may fear judgment, stigma, or retaliation, making it difficult for them to come forward. As a society, it is crucial that we break this silence, fostering an environment where survivors feel safe to share their experiences.

Understanding the Dynamics: To combat domestic abuse effectively, it is imperative to delve into the intricate dynamics that contribute to its perpetuation. As a criminal psychologist, my professional lens allows me to explore the underlying factors, shedding light on the complexities of the criminal mindset and the psychopathy that may drive such behaviour.

From Awareness to Action: Awareness alone is not enough; it must be a catalyst for tangible change. Public events, lectures, and discussions play a pivotal role in disseminating information and challenging societal norms that enable domestic abuse to persist. By fostering a culture of empathy and support, we can empower individuals to recognise, report, and escape abusive situations.

Conclusion: Domestic abuse remains a pervasive and horrendous reality, casting a long shadow over the lives of millions. To combat this epidemic, we must collectively confront the silence that shrouds it, fostering understanding, empathy, and a commitment to action. Only by illuminating the dark corners where abuse thrives can we hope to break the chains that bind victims and survivors, allowing them to reclaim their life, to rebuild a life that was taken from them.

Navigating the Holidays: The Strain and Stress of Living with Coercive Controlling Behaviour

As we approach the festive season, many of us eagerly anticipate the joy and warmth that come with the holidays. However, for some individuals, this time of year can be particularly challenging, especially when living with coercive controlling behaviour. In this blog post, we'll explore the unique strains and stresses that individuals facing such circumstances may encounter during the Christmas season.

Understanding Coercive Controlling Behaviour:

Before delving into the holiday-specific challenges, let's briefly recap what coercive controlling behaviour entails. It involves a pattern of behaviours used by one person to exert control over another through intimidation, isolation, degradation, and manipulation. Such behaviours can significantly impact the mental and emotional well-being of those experiencing them.

The Festive Strain:

Isolation During Celebrations: Coercive control often involves isolating individuals from their support networks. This isolation can intensify during the holidays when social gatherings are common.

Victims may find themselves unable to participate in celebrations with friends and family, leading to feelings of loneliness and despair.

Financial Control: The financial strain of the holidays can exacerbate the challenges faced by those experiencing coercive control. Controlling partners may restrict access to funds or dictate how money is spent, making it difficult for victims to engage in typical holiday activities or purchase gifts for loved ones.

Pressure to Conform: The holiday season comes with societal expectations and traditions. Victims of coercive control may feel an added layer of stress as they navigate these expectations while trying to appease their controlling partners. The fear of repercussions for not conforming can be overwhelming.

Coping Strategies:

- Reach Out for Support: If it's safe to do so, seek support from friends, family, or helplines. Connecting with others can provide emotional relief and a sense of solidarity.

- Create a Safety Plan: Develop a safety plan tailored to your situation. This may involve identifying safe spaces, emergency contacts, and strategies for de-escalating tense situations.

- Self-Care Practices: Prioritise self-care during the holidays. Whether it's reading, listening to music, or engaging in activities you enjoy, taking time for yourself is crucial for maintaining mental well-being.

Conclusion:

Living with coercive controlling behaviour during the holidays can be exceptionally challenging, but it's essential to remember that support is available. By understanding the unique strains faced during this season and implementing coping strategies, individuals can navigate these difficult circumstances with resilience. If you or someone you know is experiencing coercive control, reaching out for help is a crucial step toward breaking free from the cycle of abuse.

Gaslighting: Recognising the World of Difference from Everyday Disagreements

In our daily lives, disagreements are an inevitable part of human interactions. Whether it's within the family, among friends, or in the workplace, differing opinions are natural and healthy in fostering constructive discussions. However, there exists a dangerous and manipulative tactic known as gaslighting, which is vastly different from the ordinary disagreements we encounter. Gaslighting is a form of psychological manipulation that can have severe consequences on a person's mental well being. Understanding the distinction between regular disagreements and gaslighting is essential in safeguarding ourselves and promoting healthy relationships.

What is Gaslighting?

Gaslighting is a term derived from the 1944 film "Gaslight," in which the main character manipulates his wife to make her doubt her sanity. In real life, gaslighting involves one person systematically undermining another's perceptions, memories, and beliefs to gain control over them. The gaslighter may use various tactics, such as denial, distortion, contradiction, and outright lies, to sow seeds of doubt in the victim's mind and make them question their own reality.

The Tell-Tale Signs of Gaslighting Recognising gaslighting can be challenging, as it often starts subtly and progressively escalates. However, some common signs can help identify this toxic behaviour:

Discrediting: The gaslighter dismisses the victim's thoughts and feelings, making them feel their emotions are invalid or unimportant.

Constant denial: The gaslighter denies ever saying or doing things, even when evidence proves otherwise, making the victim question their memory.

Twisting the truth: Gaslighters manipulate events or conversations to make the victim doubt their interpretation of reality.

Isolation: The gaslighter may isolate the victim from friends, family, or support networks, making it easier to maintain control.

Projection: The gaslighter projects their flaws or behaviours onto the victim, making them feel as if they are the ones at fault.

Differences Between Everyday Disagreements and Gaslighting

- Intent: In regular disagreements, individuals express differing opinions with the intent to find common ground or reach a resolution. Gaslighting, on the other hand, is a deliberate manipulation tactic aimed at exerting control over the victim.

- **Reciprocity:** In typical disagreements, both

parties engage in a healthy exchange of ideas, with each person listening and respecting the other's viewpoint. In gaslighting, there is an inherent power imbalance, with one person seeking to dominate and control the other.

- **Respectful Communication:** Everyday disagreements may involve strong emotions, but they usually involve respectful communication. Gaslighting is characterised by emotional abuse, aiming to destabilise the victim's self-confidence.

- **Learning and Growth:** Constructive disagreements can foster personal growth and understanding, as individuals learn from each other's perspectives. Gaslighting, however, stifles personal growth and can lead to long lasting emotional damage.

- **Frequency and Intensity:** Regular disagreements occur sporadically and do not cause a lasting impact on mental health.

Gaslighting is persistent and can lead to anxiety, depression, and a sense of powerlessness in the victim.

Conclusion

Understanding the world of difference between

everyday disagreements and gaslighting is crucial for maintaining healthy relationships and promoting emotional well-being. Gaslighting is a manipulative and abusive tactic that seeks to control and dominate the victim through psychological means. Recognising the signs of gaslighting empowers individuals to protect themselves from emotional harm and seek support when needed. By fostering open, respectful, and constructive communication, we can create an environment where disagreements can be addressed without resorting to harmful tactics.

The Lasting Sting: Exploring the Long-Term Effects of Negging

In the world of dating and relationships, tactics to attract or manipulate others have evolved over time. One such strategy that has gained notoriety is "negging," a technique that involves giving backhanded compliments, or subtle insults to undermine a person's self-esteem. While negging might seem like a harmless flirtatious move, its long term effects can be damaging and enduring.

In this blog, we'll delve into the psychological and emotional repercussions of negging on individuals and relationships.

Understanding Negging

Negging is often employed as a manipulative strategy to gain the upper hand in a romantic interaction. Proponents of negging believe that by subtly criticising a person's appearance or behaviour, they can create a sense of insecurity, making the person more receptive to their advances. However, this approach is rooted in psychological manipulation and can have profound consequences for the targeted individual's self-esteem and overall well-being.

The Psychological Impact

- Lowered Self-Esteem: Negging chips away at a person's self-confidence by making them doubt their worth. Repeated exposure to negative comments can lead to a diminished sense of self, causing long-lasting feelings of inadequacy.

- Insecurity: Over time, those who have been subjected to negging may develop a heightened sense of insecurity about their appearance, personality, or abilities. This insecurity can spill over into other areas of their life, affecting their relationships, work, and social interactions.

- Negative Self-Image: The negative comments associated with negging can contribute to a distorted self-perception. Individuals may internalise these comments, leading to a skewed view of themselves and a perpetuation of negative self-talk.

• Trust Issues: Experiencing negging can erode trust in others. Victims may become wary of compliments or feedback, fearing that they might hide manipulative intentions.

The Impact on Relationships

• Unhealthy Dynamics: In relationships that begin with negging, power imbalances and unhealthy dynamics can take root. The recipient of negging may feel a need to constantly seek approval from their partner, creating an unhealthy dependence.

• Communication Breakdown: Effective communication is essential in any relationship, but negging undermines open and honest dialogue. Partners who have been negged may fear expressing their true thoughts or feelings, leading to misunderstandings and resentment.

• Emotional Distance: Over time, the emotional toll of negging can create a growing emotional distance between partners. Resentment and unresolved issues can fester, weakening the emotional connection.

- Cycle of Manipulation: Negging can set the stage for a cycle of manipulation within a relationship. The victim may internalise the belief that they need to please their partner to avoid criticism, perpetuating an unhealthy pattern.

Breaking Free from the Cycle - While the effects of negging can be long-lasting, individuals have the power to overcome its negative impact and rebuild their self-esteem.

Here are some steps to consider:

1. Recognise the Behaviour: Acknowledge that negging is a form of manipulation and not a healthy or genuine way to build a connection.

2. Seek Support: Reach out to friends, family, or a mental health professional who can provide guidance and help restore your self-esteem.

3. Set Boundaries: In relationships, establish clear boundaries and communicate your expectations for respectful and healthy interactions.

4. Practice Self-Compassion: Cultivate self-love and self-compassion. Focus on your strengths, accomplishments, and positive qualities.

5. Choose Healthy Relationships: Prioritise relationships built on mutual respect, open communication, and genuine affection. Surround yourself with people who uplift and support you.

Conclusion

Negging may offer temporary gratification for those who employ it, but its long-term effects on individuals and relationships are far from benign. Recognising the manipulative nature of negging is the first step toward breaking free from its grasp. By cultivating self-esteem, setting boundaries, and seeking healthy connections, individuals can rebuild their self-worth and pave the way for fulfilling and emotionally nourishing relationships. Remember, genuine connections are built on respect, trust, and a sincere appreciation for each other's unique qualities.

The Lethal Reality of Non-Fatal Strangulation: The Thin Line Between Life and Death

While many people associate strangulation with lethal intent and criminality, it is essential to understand that even non-fatal strangulation can have severe consequences. Though non-fatal strangulation may not directly result in death, it poses an alarming risk of causing unintended fatalities due to its potential to escalate into murder. This article delves into the physiological mechanisms involved in strangulation, shedding light on how seemingly non-lethal actions can easily turn fatal. Understanding the deadly ramifications of non-fatal strangulation can help raise awareness and prompt necessary actions to address this dangerous issue.

The Devastating Effects of Strangulation on the Body

Strangulation primarily targets the carotid arteries and jugular blood vessels in the neck, two vital conduits that supply blood to the brain. Direct compression of the carotid arteries leads to a decrease or loss of cerebral blood flow, resulting in brain death. Similarly, compression of the jugular blood vessels can cause quick death by producing cerebral hypoxia, leading to a loss of muscle tone and further exacerbating the pressure on the carotid arteries and trachea.

Consequences of Non-Fatal Strangulation

Non-fatal strangulation can have severe and long-lasting consequences on the victim's health, both physically and psychologically. The direct pressure on the carotid sinuses can cause a significant drop in blood pressure, leading to bradycardia and other arrhythmias. This lack of blood flow to the brain can result in anoxic and hypoxic brain injuries, leading to cognitive impairment, memory loss, and other neurological deficits.

The Precarious Line between Life and Death

Perhaps the most alarming aspect of non-fatal strangulation is how easily it can escalate into a fatal incident. As mentioned earlier, only 11 lbs of pressure applied to both carotid arteries for a mere 10 seconds are enough to cause unconsciousness. Likewise, just 4.4 lbs of pressure applied to the jugular for 10 seconds can lead to unconsciousness, while 33 lbs of pressure on the trachea is required to completely close it off. A man's handshake has between 98- 117 lbs of pressure, it shows how easily fatalities can happen.

These seemingly small amounts of pressure and short durations can rapidly turn a non-lethal act into a tragic and irreversible incident. In the heat of the moment, an assailant may not be aware of the lethal potential of their actions, leading to unintended fatalities.

In the case of jugular compression, the victim experiences cerebral hypoxia, which can cause unconsciousness. Furthermore, compromised muscle tone puts additional pressure on the carotid arteries and trachea, further increasing the risk of fatal consequences.

The Legal Perspective

Recognising the deadly potential of non-fatal strangulation, many jurisdictions have taken measures to address this issue. In several places, non-fatal strangulation has been criminalised, with penalties depending on the severity and intent of the act. These legal measures are aimed at deterring individuals from engaging in such dangerous behaviour and holding perpetrators accountable for their actions.

Conclusion

Non-fatal strangulation is far from a harmless act; it carries the potential to transform into a life-threatening situation rapidly. Understanding the physiological mechanisms involved in strangulation can help raise awareness about the dangers posed by seemingly non-lethal actions. It is crucial to continue spreading awareness about the consequences of non-fatal strangulation and to strengthen legal measures to protect potential victims. By shedding light on this issue, we can work towards creating a safer society for everyone.

Unveiling the Dark Connection: Coercive Control and Abuse, Violence and Murder

Behind the curtain of gender-based violence and murder, lies a sinister force known as coercive control. Often, this insidious form of abuse remains concealed, deeply rooted in power imbalances, and inflicted upon the vulnerable, primarily affecting females with male perpetrators.

However, it is crucial to recognise that coercive control transcends gender, culture, age, and financial status.

Understanding Coercive Control:

Coercive control is a pattern of behaviours used by an abuser to gain power and control over their victim. It involves a systematic manipulation of the victim's thoughts, emotions, and actions, leading to a loss of autonomy and independence. Perpetrators use various tactics, such as isolation, intimidation, gaslighting, financial control, and threats, to instill fear and dominance in their victims.

The Connection to Female Abuse, Violence, and Murder:

While coercive control affects individuals of all genders, it disproportionately targets females. The dynamic of male perpetrators and female victims is prevalent, largely due to historical gender inequalities and societal norms. Such controlling behaviour manifests in different forms of abuse, including physical, emotional, sexual, and financial, leading to a grim escalation of violence and, in the worst cases, murder.

Statistics and Real-Life Cases:

Tragically, the statistics reflect the harrowing reality of female abuse, violence, and murder stemming from coercive control.

Studies show that intimate partner violence accounts for a significant percentage of female homicides worldwide. Real-life cases, like that of Jane Doe*, whose life was claimed by her abusive partner, highlight the fatal consequences of coercive control.

Breaking the Gender Stereotype:

It is essential to emphasise that while most reported cases involve male perpetrators and female victims, the impact of coercive control transcends gender. Men can also be victims of abuse, facing similar manipulation and controlling tactics from their partners. Breaking the silence surrounding male victims is crucial in addressing the issue comprehensively.

Coercive Control Across Cultures:

Coercive control knows no cultural boundaries. While its manifestations may vary across different societies, the essence remains consistent, the enforcement of dominance and power. By acknowledging the universality of this issue, we can collaborate globally to find solutions and support survivors.

Coercive Control's Influence on All Ages:

This insidious form of abuse can affect individuals at any stage of life. From young adults in toxic relationships to elderly individuals facing mistreatment from caregivers, coercive control can manifest in diverse settings. Raising awareness of the signs and supporting victims across all age groups is vital in combating this menace.

The Impact Regardless of Financial Status:

Coercive control does not discriminate based on financial status. It can occur in affluent households as well as those facing economic hardship. Financial abuse, a component of coercive control, can exacerbate the victim's vulnerability, trapping them in a cycle of dependence.

Conclusion:

Coercive control remains at the core of female abuse, violence, and murder, perpetuating a vicious cycle of suffering. However, we must remember that this issue extends beyond gender, affecting individuals from all backgrounds. By fostering a society that recognizes the signs of coercive control and offers support without judgment, we can pave the way for a safer, more equal world.

Breaking free from the chains of coercive control requires collective effort, education, and empathy. Let us stand together, united against this malevolent force, and empower survivors to reclaim their lives, regardless of gender, culture, age, or financial status.
*Name changed to protect privacy.

The Understated Reality: Males as Victims of Domestic Violence and Coercive Control

When we think of domestic violence, society's immediate image is often that of a female victim suffering at the hands of a male perpetrator. While this is a tragically common and well-documented dynamic, the conversation often overlooks a significant and equally distressing reality: men can, and do, fall victim to domestic violence and coercive control. The reluctance to recognize males as victims has left countless men suffering in silence, marginalized by a system and society that doesn't always fully understand or accept their experiences.

The Hidden Truth About Male Victims

Men make up a substantial proportion of domestic violence victims. In the UK, it is estimated that one in three victims of domestic abuse is male (often abuse is not reported). Despite this, male victims are often dismissed, their experiences belittled, or worse, ignored entirely. The societal expectation that men must be strong, unemotional, and resilient can make it even harder for them to acknowledge or report abuse. Many feel trapped by the stigma associated with being a male victim, fearing they will be disbelieved or perceived as weak for not being able to "handle" their situation.

This societal stereotype, that men should be able to stand up for themselves, dismisses the true nature of domestic violence and coercive control. It is not about physical strength but psychological manipulation, emotional abuse, and systematic degradation. Abuse can take many forms beyond physical violence, such as emotional blackmail, financial control, isolation, and relentless criticism, all of which are tools that abusers, regardless of gender, use to dominate and control their partners.

The Unseen Impact of Coercive Control on Men

Coercive control, the invisible thread that binds victims in abusive relationships, is an insidious form of psychological manipulation. It often manifests through jealousy, control over daily activities, monitoring, and threats. For men, the effects of coercive control can be especially difficult to navigate, as they may feel that admitting to being controlled by a partner contradicts their societal role as a "protector."

Male victims of coercive control can face a unique set of challenges. They may endure gaslighting, where their partner manipulates them into doubting their own reality, and are often isolated from friends, family, or support systems. Over time, this can erode a man's self-esteem, sense of self-worth, and ability to trust his own judgement.

Additionally, abusers may use children as pawns, exploiting a father's emotional bond with his kids. In situations where the abusive partner threatens to take the children away, or falsely accuses the father of being abusive, many men feel helpless, trapped in a system that they feel favours women as primary caregivers.

Why Male Victims Don't Speak Up

The reasons men don't come forward are deeply entrenched in social expectations and cultural stigma. Fear of disbelief is a major barrier. When male victims muster the courage to seek help, they are often met with scepticism or even ridicule. Some have reported being asked whether they are the true perpetrator or have been advised to "man up" and handle the situation themselves.

Beyond societal stigma, there are also systemic barriers. Men seeking refuge in domestic violence shelters often find that services are overwhelmingly designed with female victims in mind. Many areas lack adequate shelters for men or the resources available are scarce. This lack of support infrastructure can leave men feeling as though there is nowhere for them to turn.

Recognising the Signs: A Shift in Perspective

To better understand and support male victims of the many forms of domestic violence and coercive control, a significant cultural shift is required. It's crucial that professionals in law enforcement, healthcare, and social services are trained to recognize the signs of abuse in men and treat their claims with the same seriousness and empathy as those of female victims.

Public awareness campaigns must broaden their scope to include the male perspective. Domestic violence does not discriminate based on gender, and neither should the services designed to support victims.

Moving Towards Change

To change the narrative, we must start by acknowledging that men can and do suffer from domestic violence and coercive control, and their experiences are just as valid and devastating as those of female victims.

Raising awareness, both in the media and within support services, is crucial to breaking down the harmful stereotypes that prevent male victims from coming forward. Support networks, legal protections, and mental health services need to be inclusive, offering men safe spaces where they feel heard, believed, and empowered to seek help. By fostering an environment that understands the complexities of abuse, regardless of the victim's gender, we can begin to dismantle the silence surrounding male victimhood and move toward a more inclusive approach to domestic violence awareness and prevention.

The Eye That Never Sleeps

We are diving into a topic that concerns the darker side of human behaviour. We'll explore the unsettling world of stalking, often referred to as "The Eye that Never Sleeps." As we unravel this subject, my goal is to provide you with valuable insights that can help you stay safe and informed.

Understanding the Stalker's Mindset

Stalking is not a new phenomenon, but it has evolved with the digital age, making it even more invasive. To protect ourselves, it's crucial to comprehend the mindset of a stalker. Delving into the intricacies of the human mind, particularly those that drive individuals to engage in such disturbing behaviour.

Stalkers often exhibit traits associated with psychopathy, obsession, and a distorted sense of entitlement. It's essential to recognise these red flags early on to protect ourselves and our loved ones. Particularly when it is not in association with domestic abuse or an intimate partner relationship.

The Eight Tiers: From Intrusion to Danger

A developed framework that classifies stalking behaviours into eight tiers, ranging from mild intrusion to potential danger. Understanding these tiers can empower you to assess and respond to situations effectively.

Each tier represents a different level of threat and recognising them early can be a key to preventing escalation.

Embracing Technological Vigilance

In our hyperconnected world, technology has become both a boon and a bane. Stalkers often exploit it to invade our privacy. From social media to location tracking, understanding how technology can be misused is crucial.

Implementing privacy settings, being mindful of what you share online, and regularly reviewing your digital footprint are essential steps in safeguarding yourself.

Stalking Prevention Strategies

Now that we've touched on the psychology and technology aspects, let's delve into practical strategies for preventing and addressing stalking:

1. Trust Your Instincts: If something feels off, it probably is. Listen to your instincts and take action if you sense danger. Do not make excuses or put

things down to coincidence, if it is out of the ordinary take notice.

2.	Maintain Privacy: Be cautious about sharing personal information online and offline. Restrict access to your social media profiles and regularly review your privacy settings. Be vigilant about what your friends and family are posting about you.

3.	Document Everything: If you suspect you're being stalked, keep a detailed record of incidents. This documentation can be crucial for legal proceedings and obtaining a restraining order. Any witnesses and their contact details will also be important, location, time, etc.

4.	Inform Trusted Individuals: Share your concerns with close friends, family, and colleagues. Having a support system is vital during such challenging times.

If people you are speaking to are dismissive, speak to somebody else. The National Stalking Helpline, Victim Support, or one of the specialized charities.

5.	Seek Professional Help: Consult with law enforcement and legal professionals to understand your options. They can guide you on obtaining a restraining order and taking legal action, this is a long process, so keeping your evidence log and keeping yourself safe is the priority.

6. Prevention of the Escalation to physical violence is very important, as a stalker becomes more confident and more devious, they are more likely to become physically violent and/or verbally abusive.

Conclusion

The Eye that Never Sleeps can be unsettling, but knowledge is our best defense. By understanding the mindset of a stalker, recognising the red flags, and implementing practical strategies, we can do our best to protect ourselves from potential harm. Stay vigilant, stay informed, and prioritise your safety. They will not stop, by just ignoring them, you have to be proactive in your own defense. Identifying the threat early is vitally important. Once identified, then act, report it and tell others, awareness, knowledge and community are keys to undermining the power of a stalker.

The Silent Menace: Unravelling the Danger of Stranger Stalking in the UK

In the realm of criminal psychology and the study of aberrant behaviour, one aspect that often goes underestimated and underfunded is the peril of stranger stalking. This insidious phenomenon, although less acknowledged than its more familiar counterparts, poses a significant threat to the safety and well-being of individuals in the UK. In this article, we delve into the reasons why stranger stalking is incredibly dangerous and why it deserves more attention and resources.

The Unseen Threat:

While stalking itself is a fairly widely recognised issue, the subtleties of stranger stalking often escape public awareness. Unlike cases where the stalker is known to the victim, stranger stalking involves an unknown assailant who fixates on an individual, monitoring their every move from the shadows. This clandestine approach makes it more difficult for victims to detect the threat, leading to delayed responses and increased danger.

Underestimated Impact:

The psychological toll of stranger stalking is profound, causing victims to live in constant fear and anxiety. The lack of familiarity with the perpetrator adds an extra layer of vulnerability, as victims are unable to predict or comprehend the motives behind the stalking. The fear of the unknown can lead to severe emotional distress, affecting not only the mental well-being of the victim but also their ability to carry out daily activities.

Underfunded Support Systems:

Stranger stalking victims often find themselves navigating a system that is ill-equipped to handle the nuances of their situation. Support services and resources dedicated to helping individuals facing this unique form of stalking are significantly underfunded. The lack of awareness and funding leaves victims without the proper assistance they need to cope with the trauma and protect themselves effectively.

The Importance of Recognition:

Recognising the severity of stranger stalking is the first step towards addressing this silent menace. Law enforcement agencies, mental health professionals, and the public at large need to be educated about the distinct characteristics of stranger stalking cases. This awareness can lead to improved prevention, intervention, and support measures.

Closing Thoughts:

In the intricate web of criminal psychology and societal safety, the danger of stranger stalking cannot be understated. By acknowledging the unique challenges posed by this form of stalking and allocating the necessary resources to combat it, we can hope to create a safer environment for individuals across the UK. It is imperative that we elevate the conversation surrounding stranger stalking, providing a voice to victims and ensuring that their experiences are not overlooked or underestimated.

Unveiling the Hidden Horror: The Urgent Need to Take Stalking Seriously

Stalking, a crime often underestimated and overlooked, demands our immediate attention and action. In this article, we will explore five compelling reasons why it is crucial to recognize and address stalking as the serious and horrific crime that it is.

Psychological Impact on Victims:

Stalking leaves deep emotional scars on its victims. The constant fear, anxiety, and emotional distress inflicted upon individuals subjected to stalking are profound. By acknowledging the psychological toll, we emphasize the need for empathy and support for those enduring such traumatic experiences.

Escalation Potential:

One of the most alarming aspects of stalking is its potential to escalate into more violent crimes. Numerous cases have shown that stalking can be a precursor to assault or even murder. Taking stalking seriously allows for early intervention, preventing the progression of such dangerous behaviours and protecting potential victims.

Violation of Privacy:

Stalking is an insidious invasion of privacy, a persistent and unwarranted intrusion into a person's personal space. Recognising stalking as a violation of one's fundamental right to privacy underscores the importance of preserving individual autonomy and security in our society.

Impact on Daily Life:

Beyond the emotional turmoil, stalking disrupts every facet of a person's daily life. The constant fear and surveillance affect a victim's ability to work, socialise, and maintain relationships. By understanding the significant disruptions caused by stalking, we emphasize the urgency of implementing legal and societal measures to address and prevent such intrusions.

Prevention of Recurrence:

Taking stalking seriously is a powerful deterrent. By sending a clear message that society will not tolerate such behaviours, we create an environment that discourages potential stalkers. This awareness encourages victims to report incidents promptly, allowing authorities to intervene and prevent the recurrence of stalking, thereby safeguarding individuals from further harm.

Conclusion:

Stalking is a silent crime that thrives in the shadows, often unnoticed until it's too late. It is imperative that we collectively raise awareness about the severity of stalking and advocate for its recognition as a horrific crime. By understanding the psychological impact, acknowledging the escalation potential, recognising the violation of privacy, addressing the daily life disruptions, and emphasizing prevention, we can work towards a society that takes stalking seriously and prioritizes the safety and well-being of its members. Together, let us unveil the hidden horror of stalking and ensure that no one suffers in silence.

Unveiling the Shadows: Shedding Light on Domestic Abuse

Domestic abuse is a sinister force that thrives in the shadows, silently wreaking havoc on the lives of countless individuals. It transforms what should be havens of love and security into landscapes of pain, fear, and anxiety. This pervasive issue is often concealed from public view, trapping victims in a cycle of suffering. The 2019-20 Crime Survey for England and Wales (CSEW) sheds light on the alarming scope of this problem, estimating that 2.3 million people experienced domestic abuse in the preceding year.

The Silent Struggle:

At the heart of domestic abuse lies a tragic transformation of intimate relationships into breeding grounds for anguish. Victims and survivors, entangled in these toxic dynamics, face the challenge of navigating a reality that contradicts the very essence of what a home should be. The silent struggle they endure often goes unnoticed, concealed behind closed doors

The Statistics Speak Volumes:

The CSEW figures underscore the magnitude of the issue, emphasizing that domestic abuse is not an isolated problem but a widespread societal concern. As we grapple with the enormity of 2.3 million people impacted in just one year, it becomes evident that this is an epidemic that demands our attention and collective action.

Breaking the Silence:

One of the greatest barriers to addressing domestic abuse is the shroud of silence that envelops it. Victims may fear judgment, stigma, or retaliation, making it difficult for them to come forward. As a society, it is crucial that we break this silence, fostering an environment where survivors feel safe to share their experiences.

Understanding the Dynamics:

To combat domestic abuse effectively, it is imperative to delve into the intricate dynamics that contribute to its perpetuation. Shedding light on the complexities of the criminal mindset and the psychopathy that may drive such behaviour.

From Awareness to Action:

Awareness alone is not enough; it must be a catalyst for tangible change. Public events, lectures, and discussions play a pivotal role in disseminating information and challenging societal norms that enable domestic abuse to persist. By fostering a culture of empathy and support, we can empower individuals to recognize, report, and escape abusive situations.

Conclusion:

Domestic abuse remains a pervasive and horrendous reality, casting a long shadow over the lives of millions. To combat this epidemic, we must collectively confront the silence that shrouds it, fostering understanding, empathy, and a commitment to action. Only by illuminating the dark corners where abuse thrives can we hope to break the chains that bind victims and survivors, allowing them to reclaim their lives and rebuild what was unjustly taken from them.

Understanding and Overcoming Unhelpful Linguistics for Stalking Victims

Delving into a crucial topic that often goes unnoticed—the impact of language on stalking victims. As someone deeply immersed in the realm of criminal psychology, I find it essential to address the harmful rhetoric that surrounds individuals facing the distressing reality of being stalked.

The Weight of Unhelpful Words

Stalking is a serious and traumatic experience that can leave victims feeling isolated and vulnerable. Unfortunately, well-intentioned individuals sometimes unknowingly contribute to the distress by using language that minimises or dismisses the severity of the situation. Let's explore a few common phrases and why they can be so unhelpful.

"Why don't you just change your routine?"

This suggestion oversimplifies the complexity of stalking. Changing routines may not always be practical or effective, and it places the burden on the victim rather than addressing the perpetrator's inappropriate behaviou

"You're overreacting."

Dismissing someone's feelings as an overreaction diminishes the emotional toll stalking can take. Validating the victim's emotions and concerns is crucial for fostering a supportive environment.

"Just ignore it, and it will go away."

Stalking is not a situation that typically resolves itself through neglect. Ignoring it may escalate the danger and ignores the need for proper intervention and support.

"Maybe they're just lonely and want attention."

Attributing stalking behaviour to benign motives

minimises the seriousness of the situation.

Stalking is a criminal act, and its root cause lies in the perpetrator's unhealthy fixation rather than benign loneliness.

"What were you wearing? Did you lead them on?"

Blaming the victim's behaviour or appearance perpetuates harmful stereotypes. Stalking is about control and power, and no one should be held responsible for the actions of a stalker.

Empathy and Education.

It's crucial to replace unhelpful language with empathy and education. Here are alternative ways to approach conversations with stalking victims:

1. Offer Supportive Statements:

    "I'm here for you."

    "Your feelings are valid, and I believe you."

2. Encourage Professional Help:

    "It's important to involve law enforcement."

    "Seeking counselling can provide valuable support."

3. Raise Awareness:

"Stalking is a criminal act, and no one deserves to experience it."

"Let's work together to raise awareness about stalking."

4. Educate Others:

"It's crucial to understand the impact of stalking on victims."

"Let's promote empathy and awareness in our community."

Conclusion

Language matters, especially when dealing with sensitive topics like stalking. As we strive to create a more supportive and informed society, let's be mindful of the words we use and work together to empower and uplift those who have experienced the trauma of stalking. Stay informed, stay empathetic, and make a positive difference in the lives of stalking victims.

Navigating Co-Dependency: Unveiling the Complexities of Seeking Control in Romantic Relationships

Today we are looking at unravelling the layers of co-dependency in romantic relationships, with a closer look at why some individuals, particularly females, may find themselves drawn to partners who exhibit abusive or controlling behaviours.

Understanding the Dark Side: Abusive or Controlling Partners in Co-Dependency

Co-dependency is not a one-size-fits-all concept, and its complexities often extend to the dynamics of control and abuse within relationships. Let's explore why some individuals may unconsciously seek out partners who display these troubling behaviours.

The Illusion of Security

One reason individuals, regardless of gender, may gravitate towards abusive or controlling partners is the illusion of security. In co-dependent relationships, the partner who exhibits these behaviours may initially provide a sense of structure and stability. The illusion of control can be enticing for someone who, perhaps due to past experiences, seeks a semblance of order and predictability.

Low Self-Esteem and the Desire for Validation.
For some, co-dependency is intertwined with low self-esteem. Seeking validation from a partner, even if that validation comes in the form of control, can be a way for individuals to temporarily soothe their insecurities. The abuser! s ability to exert dominance might be misconstrued as a form of love or affirmation, creating a distorted sense of value for the co- dependent individual.

The Cycle of Power and Dependency

Abusive or controlling partners often thrive on power dynamics. In co-dependent relationships, this power dynamic can create a cycle of dependency, where the victim becomes increasingly reliant on the abuser for both emotional and practical needs. Breaking free from this cycle can be challenging, as the victim may fear the consequences of asserting their independence.

Roots in Past Trauma

Understanding the roots of co-dependency involves acknowledging the impact of past traumas. Individuals who have experienced abuse or control in childhood may unknowingly gravitate towards similar dynamics in adulthood. The familiarity of these patterns, while unhealthy, can create a perverse comfort zone for those navigating co-dependency.

Breaking Free: Empowering Change

Recognising the need for an abusive or controlling partner is a crucial step towards breaking the cycle of co-dependency. Firstly, it involves acknowledging the unhealthy patterns, seeking support, and gradually reclaiming one's sense of self-worth.

Therapy, support groups, and education on healthy relationship dynamics are essential tools in this journey. It's important to remember that everyone deserves a relationship built on respect, communication, and genuine care. If you or someone you know is experiencing an abusive relationship, reaching out to professional resources or helplines can provide the necessary guidance and support.

In conclusion, the intertwining of co-dependency and abusive or controlling partners is a complex issue rooted in the quest for security, validation, and the cycle of power and dependency. By shedding light on these dynamics, we empower individuals to break free from harmful patterns and cultivate relationships that foster growth, respect, and true connection. As always, feel free to share your thoughts or experiences in the comments below.

Silent Shadows: Unmasking the Tell Tale Signs of Stalking

Taking a look into the intriguing realm of criminal psychology. Shedding a light on a topic that often goes unnoticed until it's too late – how victims recognize they are being stalked. Stalking is a pervasive issue that can affect anyone, and understanding the signs is crucial for early intervention. So, let's explore the subtle indicators that victims may pick up on.

What is stalking?

In England & Wales, a precise legal definition of stalking has never been defined. The Protection from Harassment Act 1997 does not define stalking, but rules that a person must not pursue a course of conduct that amounts to the harassment of another person.

In UK law we define stalking as repeated and unwanted by the victim, which causes the victim alarm or distress. With so many variations as to what stalking is, it can lead the victims to being confused as to what stalking is, due to differing and no solid definitions public perception of stalking differs greatly.

The Unsettling Feeling:

Stalking often begins subtly, with the victim experiencing an uneasy feeling that something isn't quite right. This intuition, while difficult to define, serves as an early warning sign. Victims may find themselves looking over their shoulder, feeling watched, or sensing an inexplicable discomfort in familiar surroundings.

Unexplained Presence:

Victims may notice a persistent and unexplained presence in their daily lives. Whether it's a stranger frequently appearing in their vicinity or a recurring face in a crowd, the feeling of being observed becomes increasingly apparent.

Unexpected Encounters:

Stalkers may orchestrate chance encounters to create a false sense of familiarity. Victims might notice the same person showing up in places they frequent, even if those locations are not easily accessible to the general public.

Excessive Contact:

Unwanted communication becomes a key indicator.

Victims may receive an excessive number of calls, texts, or emails, often at odd hours. The content of these messages might range from seemingly harmless to increasingly intrusive or threatening.

Social Media Monitoring:

In the digital age, stalking extends into the online realm. Victims may observe their stalker closely monitoring their social media accounts, liking or commenting on posts from fake or anonymous profiles.

Vandalism or Property Damage:

Physical evidence, such as damage to personal property, can be a stark sign of stalking. Victims may discover slashed tires, broken windows, or other intentional acts of vandalism that signal a targeted campaign against them.

Trusting Your Instincts:

One of the most powerful tools a victim possesses is their intuition. If something feels off, it likely is. Trusting those instincts and acknowledging the discomfort is the first step toward recognizing and addressing stalking behaviour.

Seeking Support:

Recognising stalking can be a challenging and isolating experience. Victims are encouraged to reach out to friends, family, or professionals for support. Sharing concerns and experiences can help validate their feelings and provide a network of assistance.

Reporting stalking to the police is often seen as a postcode lottery, though training is ongoing, it is still not easy to find good police support or understanding. Going via established charities such as Victim Support, The Suzie Lamplugh Trust or Alice Ruggles Trust, you have a great chance of speaking to a professional with a good understanding and ability to guide a victim through the legal maze.

Conclusion:

Understanding the signs of stalking is paramount for early intervention and prevention. By recognizing these subtle indicators, victims empower themselves to take action and seek the support they need. Let's continue to raise awareness about stalking and work towards creating a world where everyone can feel safe and secure.

Love Bombing: recognizing Red Flags in Intense Relationships

Love is a beautiful and complex emotion, but sometimes it can be exploited in ways that are not so beautiful. Love bombing is a manipulation tactic that individuals may use to establish control in a relationship. In this blog post, we will explore why it is essential to recognise the red flags associated with love bombing.

Understanding Love Bombing: Love bombing refers to an intense and overwhelming display of affection and attention in the early stages of a relationship. It can make you feel like you're on cloud nine, but it often conceals darker intentions. People who use love bombing may do so to gain power and control over their partner.

The Importance of Recognising Red Flags:

Distinguishing Genuine Love: Love bombing can make it difficult to distinguish between genuine affection and manipulation. Recognising red flags can help you differentiate between healthy and unhealthy relationships.

Avoiding Manipulative Partners: By identifying love bombing early on, you can avoid becoming entangled in a relationship with a manipulative partner who may have harmful intentions.

Protecting Your Emotional Well-being: Love bombing can take a toll on your emotional well-being. Recognising the signs allows you to protect your mental and emotional health.

Red Flags to Watch Out For:

Excessive Attention: If your partner seems too good to be true and bombards you with attention, gifts, and compliments from the start, be cautious.

Rapid Commitment: Love bombers often rush the relationship to the next level, pushing for exclusivity or even marriage prematurely.

Isolation: They may attempt to isolate you from friends and family, making you more dependent on them emotionally.

Over-the-Top Promises: Unrealistic promises and declarations of love that seem too good to be true can be a sign of love bombing.

Mood Swings: Love bombers may exhibit extreme

mood swings, alternating between intense affection and anger or jealousy.

Conclusion:

Understanding the psychology behind love bombing and its impact on relationships is invaluable. By recognising these red flags, we can protect ourselves and others from falling into potentially harmful situations. Healthy relationships are built on trust, respect, and genuine affection, not manipulative tactics like love bombing. It's essential to be aware and educated about these issues to promote safer and happier connections.

Cracking the Narcissist Code: Three Revealing Questions to Spot Them

Narcissism is a personality trait that has fascinated psychologists and the general public alike for years. The term is often used colloquially, but identifying genuine narcissistic tendencies can be a complex task. As someone deeply invested in understanding the minds of individuals with criminal tendencies, psychopathy, and other intricate aspects of the human psyche, I've come to appreciate the importance of recognising narcissism in various contexts. In this blog, we'll explore a practical and insightful approach to identifying narcissists.

We'll delve into three key questions that can serve as a compass, helping you navigate the maze of narcissistic behaviour. So, let's embark on this journey to unravel the enigma of narcissism and equip ourselves with a valuable tool for understanding those who exhibit these traits.

Do They Constantly Seek Attention and Validation?

Narcissists often exhibit a strong desire for attention and validation. This can manifest in various ways:

Excessive Self-Promotion: They may constantly talk about their achievements, talents, or qualities, seeking admiration from others.

Grandiosity: Narcissists may have an inflated sense of self-importance and expect special treatment or recognition.

Attention-Grabbing Behaviour: They might use attention-seeking behaviours like loud talking, dramatic gestures, or provocative actions to ensure all eyes are on them.

Need for Praise: They frequently seek praise,

compliments, and positive feedback to boost their self-esteem.

Are They Empathetic or Self-Absorbed?

Empathy is a crucial factor in distinguishing narcissists from others. Here's how to assess their level of empathy:

Lack of Empathy: Narcissists often struggle to genuinely understand or care about other people's feelings or needs.

Self-Centred Conversations:

Their conversations tend to revolve around themselves, their achievements, and their interests, with little interest in what others have to say.

Difficulty Sharing the Spotlight: Narcissists may become resentful when others receive attention or praise, as they believe they should always be the centre of attention.

Manipulative Behaviour: They may exploit others for personal gain without regard for the consequences.

Do They React Strongly to Criticism? The way individuals respond to criticism can reveal narcissistic tendencies:

Defensiveness: Narcissists often become defensive when criticised, even if the feedback is constructive. They may deflect blame onto others or make excuses for their behaviour.

Anger and Hostility: Criticism can trigger strong negative emotions in narcissists, leading to anger, hostility, or even retaliation against the critic.

Inability to Accept Fault: They rarely take responsibility for their mistakes and may insist that they are always right.

Dismissive Attitude: Narcissists might dismiss the critic's opinions, believing that their perspective is the only valid one.

Conclusion: Unmasking Narcissism for a Deeper Understanding. As we wrap up our exploration into the world of narcissism, it's clear that identifying these traits is not a straightforward task. The complex and often subtle nature of narcissistic behaviour can make it challenging to pinpoint. However, armed with the three revealing questions we've discussed, you're now better equipped to detect potential narcissistic tendencies in those around you.

Remember that these questions are not meant to serve as a definitive diagnosis, but as a tool for observation and understanding. They can help you navigate relationships, both personal and professional, with greater insight. By recognising narcissistic behaviour, you can make informed decisions and take appropriate steps to protect yourself and maintain healthy boundaries.

As someone passionate about unravelling the intricacies of the criminal mindset and the psychology of deviant behaviours, understanding narcissism is a valuable addition to your arsenal. It not only enhances your own safety but also contributes to a deeper comprehension of the individuals.

So, continue your journey into the human psyche and use these insights to navigate the complex world of personalities and behaviours.

The Crucial Importance of Avoiding Toxic Relationships

In our journey through life, we often seek love and companionship, but it's equally important to be vigilant and discerning when it comes to relationships. Toxic relationships can be emotionally, mentally, and even physically damaging. In my work and interests related to the criminal mindset and domestic abuse, I've come to understand the significance of recognising the signs and preventing toxic relationships. Here, we'll delve into why it's crucial to steer clear of them from the start.

Emotional and Psychological Health

Toxic relationships are notorious for taking a toll on your emotional and psychological well-being. The constant stress, negativity and manipulation can lead to anxiety, depression, and low self- esteem. In my experience discussing psychopathy and criminal behaviour, I've seen how these traits can manifest in toxic relationships, leading to long-lasting damage.

Impact on Physical Health

It might surprise some to know that toxic relationships can also have severe physical consequences. Chronic stress from such relationships can weaken the immune system, leading to various health issues. Furthermore, physical abuse can escalate in toxic relationships, putting one's safety at risk.

The Cycle of Dysfunction

Toxic relationships can become a never-ending cycle of dysfunction. Patterns of abuse, manipulation, and forgiveness repeat themselves, making it increasingly difficult to break free. I've seen how offenders can exploit these cycles to maintain control.

Prevention Is Key

The old adage, "an ounce of prevention is worth a pound of cure," couldn't be truer when it comes to toxic relationships. Recognising the warning signs early and making conscious decisions to avoid entering such relationships can save you from years of heartache and potential harm.

Red Flags to Watch Out For

As someone who has a great interest in criminal mindsets and psychopathy, I see the same red flags so many times and work to help others be aware of these certain red flags. Isolation from friends and family, constant criticism, emotional manipulation, and signs of aggression are indicators that a relationship may be toxic. It's crucial to trust your instincts and not ignore these signs. A relationship is a two-way street, give and take, not dominance and fear.

Seek Support and Counselling

If you find yourself in a toxic relationship, don't hesitate to seek help. Whether through therapy, counselling, or talking to a trusted friend or family member, reaching out is a vital step in breaking free from the cycle of dysfunction.

In conclusion, knowing and understanding the dynamics of toxic relationships sheds light on the importance of avoiding toxic relationships. Prevention is indeed the best course of action, it can save people from years of heartache, potential harm and death.

Unmasking the Silent Abuse: Understanding Coercive Controlling Behaviour

Coercive controlling behaviour is a deeply troubling form of psychological and emotional abuse that often hides in plain sight. It's insidious and its victims often suffer in silence. Delving into the world of coercive controlling behaviour, shedding light on what it is, how it manifests, and the lasting impact it has on victims.

Defining Coercive Controlling Behaviour Coercive controlling behaviour, also known as coercive control, is a pervasive pattern of behaviour where one person seeks to dominate and control another through a variety of tactics. Not just in romantic relationships; it can occur in familial, professional, and social settings.

Common Tactics of Coercive Control

1. **Isolation:** Coercive controllers isolate their victims from friends, family, and support networks, controlling who they see and where they go.

2. **Manipulation**: Emotional manipulation is a hallmark of coercive control. This includes gaslighting, constant criticism and emotional blackmail.

3. Financial Control: Abusers may control their victim's finances, making them financially dependent and trapped.

4. Surveillance: Victims are often subjected to constant monitoring, both online and offline.

5. Threats and Intimidation: Threats of violence or harm, whether directed at the victim or their loved ones, are common.

Sexual Coercion: Sex is used as a tool for control, making the victim feel obligated or forced into sexual acts.

Recognising Coercive Control

- Recognising coercive control can be challenging, because it often happens gradually. Victims may downplay or normalise the behaviour, making it hard for outsiders to spot. Some signs to watch for include:

- Drastic changes in the victim's behaviour or personality.

- Fear or unease when discussing the relationship.

- Isolation from friends and family.

- Financial dependence on the abuser.

- Feeling constantly monitored/controlled.

The Lasting Impact

The effects of coercive controlling behaviour are profound and long-lasting. Victims may experience anxiety, depression, PTSD, and a diminished sense of self-worth. It can also affect their ability to form healthy relationships in the future.

Seeking Help

If you or someone you know is experiencing coercive controlling behaviour, it's crucial to seek help. Reach out to a trusted friend, family member, or a professional counsellor. Many organisations specialise in supporting victims of domestic abuse and coercive control.

Conclusion

Coercive controlling behaviour is a grave concern that regularly affects individuals across various relationships and genders. Recognising the signs and providing support to victims is essential in breaking the cycle of abuse and helping survivors regain their autonomy and well-being.

By shedding light on this silent abuse, we can work towards creating a society where coercive control has no place, and individuals can live free from fear and manipulation.

Silent Terror: The Urgent Need to Confront Stalking in Our Communities

Stalking, often regarded as a shadowy and insidious crime, demands our immediate attention and comprehensive action from law enforcement agencies.

It's a behaviour that goes beyond the conventional

definitions of harassment, with some far reaching consequences for its victims. In this blog, we will explore five compelling reasons why the police must elevate their response to stalking cases, acknowledging the potential for escalation, the profound psychological trauma inflicted on victims, the evolving role of technology, the disruptive impact on daily life, and the critical need for consistent legal consequences.

By understanding these facets, we can begin to appreciate the urgency of taking stalking more seriously and the crucial role of the police in safeguarding potential victims and our communities at large.

Potential for Escalation: Stalking is often a precursor to more severe crimes, including domestic violence and murder. Research shows that a significant number of domestic violence cases have a history of stalking. By recognizing and addressing stalking early, the police can intervene before the situation escalates into a tragedy. For instance, studies have revealed that in cases of intimate partner violence, stalking behaviours often precede physical violence.

Identifying and responding to these early signs is essential to protect potential victims.

Psychological Trauma: Stalking victims endure

substantial psychological trauma. The constant fear, anxiety, and sense of helplessness can lead to severe mental health issues such as anxiety disorders, depression, and post- traumatic stress disorder (PTSD). Victims often experience sleep disturbances, loss of concentration, and paranoia, significantly impacting their daily lives and overall well-being. Police acknowledging this trauma is critical for providing the necessary support and empathy to victims.

Technology's Role: In our digital age, stalking has evolved to include cyberstalking.

Perpetrators use technology to harass their victims, which can be just as distressing and damaging as physical stalking. Police need to stay up-to-date with the latest methods used by cyberstalkers. This includes understanding how social media platforms can be used for harassment, recognising the signs of GPS tracking through smartphones and investigating

online threats. Training in digital forensics and cybercrime investigation is crucial to effectively combat cyberstalking.

Impact on Daily Life: Stalking can disrupt every aspect of a victim's life. To escape their stalker, victims may need to change their daily routines, relocate, or even go into hiding. Many are forced to quit jobs or educational pursuits to protect themselves.

This disruption to their daily lives can have a lasting impact on their financial stability and quality of life. Moreover, the fear of being stalked can result in social isolation, as victims may withdraw from friends and family to avoid putting them at risk. Recognising these profound disruptions in victims' lives underscore the urgency of police intervention.

Legal Consequences: Stalking is a crime in many jurisdictions, with specific laws in place to prosecute offenders. However, these laws are often underutilised or not enforced rigorously.

Police need specialised training to recognise stalking behaviours, gather the necessary evidence, and support victims through the legal process. Furthermore, consistent enforcement of restraining orders and monitoring of convicted stalkers is crucial to ensuring the safety of victims. Collaborative efforts with the legal system and victim advocacy organisations are essential to streamline the legal consequences for stalkers.

In summary, stalking is a complex and deeply harmful behaviour that requires a multifaceted response from law enforcement. Recognising the potential for escalation, the psychological trauma inflicted on victims, the role of technology, the disruptive impact on daily life, and the legal consequences of stalking are all vital aspects of taking this issue more seriously. Police must be well-trained, empathetic, and proactive in addressing stalking to protect potential victims and prevent further harm.

Unravelling the Appeal: Why Women Are Attracted to Bad Boys

The age-old question of why some women are drawn to "bad boys" has sparked numerous debates and discussions, as well as many song lyrics, films, books and dramas. It is a topic that has piqued the curiosity of psychologists, sociologists, and relationship experts and writers alike. Contrary to conventional beliefs, the attraction to "bad boys" may not be as irrational as it seems. In this article, we will delve into the psychological and sociological aspects that shed light on why some women find themselves irresistibly drawn to these enigmatic and often troubled characters.

The Allure of Confidence

One of the most significant reasons women find bad boys attractive lies in their innate confidence. Bad boys typically exude an air of self-assuredness and charisma, which can be highly appealing. Confidence is a universally attractive trait, and when combined with a dash of rebelliousness, it can be captivating to those seeking excitement and adventure in their lives.

The Thrill of the Unknown

Human nature often craves novelty and excitement. Bad boys, with their air of unpredictable and unconventional behaviour, introduce an element of the unknown into a woman's life. This sense of unpredictability can create a thrilling emotional rollercoaster that some find exhilarating. It is essential to remember that this thrill is not necessarily sustainable or healthy in the long term, but in the initial stages, it can be alluring.

Breaking Social Norms

Society has long dictated the ideal partner for women, often revolving around stable, caring, and nurturing attributes. However, the attraction to bad boys may, in part, stem from a desire to challenge these societal norms. Engaging with someone who is perceived as a rebel can be seen as an act of defiance and independence. It is a way of breaking away from traditional expectations and exploring personal boundaries.

The Rescuer Complex

Some women may feel an innate need to "fix" or "rescue" others, including bad boys. This rescuer complex can lead them to believe that they can positively influence the bad boy's life and bring about positive change. This nurturing instinct can become a driving force behind their attraction, despite potential warning signs of an unhealthy relationship.

Emotional Intensity

Bad boys are often characterised by their emotionally intense personalities. While this intensity can lead to tumultuous relationships, it can also create a deep emotional connection that some women crave. The emotional highs and lows experienced in such relationships can foster a sense of profound intimacy and passion, which can be hard to replicate in more stable partnerships.

Conclusion

The attraction between women and bad boys is a complex interplay of psychological, sociological, and cultural factors. The allure of confidence, the thrill of the unknown, the desire to challenge societal norms, the rescuer complex, and the emotional intensity all contribute to the appeal.

However, it is crucial to recognise that while the excitement and passion may be enticing, relationships with bad boys often come with inherent risks. It is essential for individuals to prioritise their well-being, emotional health, and safety when choosing a partner. Striking a balance between adventure and stability, excitement and reliability, is key to building a healthy and fulfilling long-term relationship.

As we continue to explore the intricacies of human relationships, understanding the motivations behind attractions, such as the affinity for bad boys, can provide valuable insights into our own behaviours and the dynamics of partnerships in contemporary society.

"Unmasking the Mystery: The Ever-Growing Fascination with Criminal Psychology and Criminology"

The intense fascination with criminology, criminal behavioural science, and criminal psychology among the general public has undeniably surged over the last four decades. This phenomenon can be attributed to a combination of factors that have made these fields captivating and accessible. Let's delve into why this fascination has grown.

Media Influence: One of the most significant drivers of public interest in criminal behaviour has been the media. Television shows like "Criminal Minds," "Mindhunter," and documentaries on infamous serial killers have brought the intricacies of criminal psychology into living rooms. These shows offer a thrilling glimpse into the minds of criminals and the professionals who study them, fuelling curiosity.

True Crime Genre: The popularity of true crime books, podcasts, and documentaries cannot be understated. They provide real-life accounts of criminal cases, investigations, and court trials.

People are drawn to the suspense and the opportunity to analyse these cases alongside experts, deepening their understanding of the criminal mind.

Internet and Social Media: The internet has democratised knowledge, allowing individuals to access information about criminology and psychology with ease. Online forums, blogs, and YouTube channels hosted by experts or enthusiasts offer a wealth of content on these subjects, making learning about criminal behaviour more accessible than ever.

Psychological Thrill: Human beings are naturally curious about the darker aspects of human nature. Understanding why someone commits a crime, especially heinous ones, can be psychologically intriguing. It gives people a sense of empowerment to decode the motives.

Relevance to Society: In an era marked by heightened awareness of safety and security, people want to understand the dynamics of crime and how to protect themselves and their communities. This has led to a surge in interest in criminal psychology and behaviour as individuals seek to comprehend the threats around them.

Academic Expansion: Over the past few decades, academic institutions have increasingly recognised the importance of criminology and criminal psychology. This has led to more comprehensive courses and programs, attracting students and scholars who, in turn, contribute to the dissemination of knowledge.

Humanising Criminals: There has been a shift in recent years towards humanising criminals in media and literature. Exploring their backgrounds and the factors that led to their criminality has made these subjects more relatable and complex, adding depth to the public's interest.

Psychological Profiling: The use of criminal profiling in real-life investigations, as seen in high profile cases, has piqued public curiosity. It showcases the practical application of psychological theories in solving crimes, which is both fascinating and educational.

In conclusion, the growing fascination with criminology, criminal behavioural science, and criminal psychology can be attributed to a combination of media influence, increased accessibility to information, a natural human curiosity about the darker aspects of human nature, and the relevance of these fields to modern society. As we continue to explore the depths of the criminal mind, it is likely that this fascination will persist and evolve in the years to come.

Part 9

True Crime Places

Armley Gaol

HMP Leeds, Armley Gaol was purpose built on a high vantage point towering over the city of Leeds, this prison opened its doors in 1847 and has been continuously home to a variety of male prisoners. There are some references to female prisoners in the early days, but no substantial official data. Categorised as a B facility which serves as a local, dispersal, remand and long term prison.

This imposing fortress was a hanging prison up to 1961 and gained a grade 2 heritage listing in 1976. The renown Victorian castle like radial architectural style was typical of the time, this one provides four wings which have three landings of cells, not much has changed internally throughout the time, other than electricity and internal plumbing. Two more wings were added in 1994.

The castle style entrance was the main gate up to 2002 when the new entrance was constructed with more staff and security facilities. The prison can house up to 1212 prisoners in six residential units, a segregation unit, First Night Centre, Vulnerable Prisoner unit and in-patients Healthcare Facility all surrounded by a substantial parameter wall.

HMP Leeds, locally known as Armley took over all the capital punishment for Yorkshire from York castle in 1896. There have only been two public hangings in Armley on the same day, that being the first held there, only one woman has been executed here and the last execution was in 1961, 4 years prior to the abolition of the death penalty nationally. In total there were 93 men and 1 condemned woman in this prison, with a variety of hangmen throughout that time.

The first and only public hangings were Sargisson, 20, who had had murdered John Cooper during a robbery near Rotherham. Despite attempting to blame an accomplice, Sargisson was found guilty and sent to the gallows.

Myers, 43, from Sheffield, had stabbed to death his wife Elizabeth in a drunken rage. According to local records, "Both were hanged outside the gaol in September 1864. The double execution, witnessed by around 80,000 people, did not go according to plan. Sargisson took several minutes to die while the throat wound Myers had attempted to kill himself in prison, opened up in the noose creating a bloody scene described by the Leeds Mercury at the time as: *"a sad and horrible picture of humanity"*. Emily Swann is the only women to be hanged at Armley she was found guilty of murdering her husband William with her lover John Gallagher. The couple were executed together on December 29, 1903.

Local records show, "Both were wearing hoods and had nooses around their neck when Swann, 42, said: "Good morning, John". Gallagher replied: "Good morning love." Swann then said: " Goodbye, God bless you" before the trapdoor opened and the two were killed.

Zsiga Pankotia was the last prisoner to be executed at Armley he was a 31 year old, Hungarian national who murdered a successful market trader in the Leeds suburb of Roundhay during a bungled burglary, in February 1961, he was executed in June 1961.

Probably the most contentious hanging in Armley was that of Alfred Moore, a chicken farmer from Huddlesfield, he was convicted and executed for shooting and killing 2 police officers at his farm in 1951.

Clifford Mead of Huddersfield who was a known criminal and suspected fence at the time, on his deathbed in 1998, produced the gun and a statement about the killing of the two police officers in 1951.

Alfred Moore, who was 36 at the time, protested his innocence right up until his execution in 1952. His children and retired detective Steve Lawson have been campaigning for a posthumous pardon.

As you walk the corridors and passage ways of this imposing prison, it is easy to imagine the pain, suffering and desolation of its inmates over the expanse of time. Just think how many stories the walls could tell.

Some former inmates:

Charles Bronson (prisoner)   Roy Chubby Brown

Adam Johnson (footballer)   Stefan Ivan Kiszko

David Oluwale   Charles Peace

John Poulson   Peter Sutcliffe

Unveiling the Enigma: The History of the Old Bailey in London

When one delves into the annals of London's criminal justice system, they're bound to encounter the enigmatic and historic Old Bailey. Situated in the heart of the city, the Old Bailey, officially known as the Central Criminal Court, has stood as an enduring symbol of justice for centuries.

A Glimpse into the Past

The Old Bailey's history dates back to the late 17th century when it was originally constructed as a Sessions House to handle the growing number of criminal trials in London. Designed by renowned architect Edward Mountford, the building's imposing facade reflects the seriousness of its purpose. It became known as the "Bailey" because it stands on the site of the medieval Newgate Gaol's bailey, or outer courtyard.

Trials and Tribulations

Over the years, the Old Bailey has witnessed some of the most infamous trials in British history. From the trial of Oscar Wilde for "gross indecency" to the prosecution of the Kray Twins for murder, its courtrooms have hosted a wide array of cases, some of which continue to captivate the public's imagination.

The Enigma of the Building

The Old Bailey's enigmatic aura extends beyond its historical significance. Its iconic dome, a distinctive feature of the London skyline, is said to have a whispering gallery where one can hear hushed conversations from across the room.

This architectural marvel adds a layer of intrigue to the already mysterious atmosphere of the courtroom.

A Personal Connection

For many like me, who have had the privilege of visiting London, The Old Bailey holds a special place in their hearts. During my recent visit to London, one of my must see places was the beautiful Dame of Justice on top of the Old Bailey. It's a landmark of the city's skyline that resonates with the pursuit of justice.

Modern Relevance

In the present day, the Old Bailey remains a vital hub of justice in London, handling a range of criminal cases, from theft to murder. Its courtrooms continue to serve as a stage for the pursuit of truth and justice.

Conclusion

The history and enigma of the Old Bailey are deeply intertwined with the evolution of the British legal system. Its architectural grandeur and storied past make it a symbol of justice and a testament to the enduring pursuit of truth in the face of crime. As you explore the criminal mindset and the psychology of offenders, the Old Bailey's rich history is a compelling chapter to examine.

Whether you're a psychologist, lecturer, or crime enthusiast the Old Bailey's story, is a fascinating piece of London's criminal justice puzzle.

Addressing Inequity in Sentencing: A Closer Look at Homicide Tariffs in England & Wales

Homicide is a tragic and devastating crime that profoundly impacts families, communities, and society at large. In England & Wales, the judicial system aims to deliver justice by imposing tariffs

fixed sentences for particular crimes. However, recent findings have shed light on potential inequities in the current homicide sentencing system, particularly when it comes to the use of weapons found in the home versus those brought from elsewhere. This article explores the existing discrepancies and the implications they may have on victims and their families.

The Current Disparity in Homicide Tariffs

Presently, in England & Wales, a notable discrepancy exists between the tariffs for murders committed using weapons found in the home and those involving weapons brought from outside. If a killer uses a weapon from the home, they may face a tariff of 15 years. Conversely, if the murder weapon is brought from elsewhere; the tariff can be 25 years or more.

This discrepancy raises concerns about fairness and justice in the judicial system. It implies that the location of the crime and the source of the weapon have a significant impact on the severity of the punishment, regardless of the heinousness of the act committed. Such disparities can potentially lead to unintended consequences, allowing perpetrators of equally brutal crimes to receive unequal sentencing based on arbitrary factors.

Understanding the Prevalence of Domestic Homicides

Research has consistently shown that a substantial

proportion of homicides occur within the context of domestic violence. Approximately one in four homicides are committed by a current or former partner, close relative, or family member. These chilling statistics highlight the urgent need for a fair and consistent approach to sentencing in cases involving domestic violence.

Implications for Victims and Families

The existing sentencing disparity may inadvertently send the wrong message to society, victims, and their families. When crimes are committed within the domestic sphere, the implication of a reduced tariff for using a weapon found in the home might inadvertently diminish the seriousness of the offence. This could be perceived as devaluing the lives lost, particularly if the victim was murdered by a family member or intimate partner.

Moreover, the current system may inadvertently discourage victims from reporting. Domestic violence or seeking help, as they might fear that their attackers could receive lenient sentences due to the weapon's origin.

Rethinking Sentencing Policies

In light of these concerns, it is crucial for policymakers and the legal system to reassess the existing homicide tariffs and work toward a more equitable and victim-centred approach. A few potential solutions could be considered:

Standardised Sentencing Guidelines:

Implementing standardised sentencing guidelines for homicide cases, irrespective of the weapon's source or the location of the crime, could help ensure consistency and fairness in the judicial process.

Focus on Intent and Severity: Shifting the focus of sentencing from the origin of the weapon or the location of the crime to the intent behind the crime and its severity would promote a more nuanced and just approach. Sentencing should be based on the heinousness of the act and the impact it has on the victim's family and the community.

Victim Impact Statements: Encouraging the use of victim impact statements during sentencing hearings can help judges better understand the true extent of the harm caused and the trauma experienced by surviving family members.

Specialised Training for Judges and Legal Professionals:

Providing specialised training for judges and legal professionals in handling domestic violence cases can enhance their understanding of the unique dynamics involved and aid in rendering appropriate sentences.

Conclusion

In conclusion, the existing disparity in homicide tariffs in England & Wales concerning the source of the weapon used and location of the crime is a matter that warrants urgent attention. Given that a significant proportion of homicides occur within the context of domestic violence, it is crucial to address these inequities to ensure that justice is served and that and their families receive the

support they deserve. By rethinking the sentencing policies and adopting a victim- centred approach, the legal system can take a significant step toward fostering a more just and equitable society.

Unmasking Jack the Ripper: A Chilling Walk Through History

In the heart of London's East End, where narrow cobbled streets whisper secrets from the past, I embarked on a journey that would reveal the dark and enigmatic character of one of history's most infamous serial killers – Jack the Ripper.

This immersive experience, known as the "Jack the Ripper Walk," not only delves into the gruesome murders but also provides a glimpse into the mind of a serial killer that continues to haunt the annals of criminal history.

A Night Time Encounter with the Shadows of the Past

As a true crime enthusiast, I've always been drawn to the darkest corners of the human psyche. So, it was only natural that I found myself on a moonlit night in Whitechapel, where the chilling events of the late 19th century unfolded.

The Jack the Ripper walk is not your typical historical tour. It's a haunting exploration into the criminal mindset, led by knowledgeable guides who have immersed themselves in the case's details. The walk takes you through the very streets where the Ripper walked and committed his heinous acts, creating an eerie atmosphere that transports you back in time.

The Mysterious Character of Jack the Ripper

What struck me most during this experience was the opportunity to delve into the character of Jack the Ripper. This elusive killer remains unidentified to this day, adding an air of mystery that continues to captivate the public's imagination. The tour delves into the psychology of the Ripper, attempting to understand the motives and methods behind the murders.

It becomes apparent that Jack the Ripper was not just a ruthless murderer, but a cunning and methodical predator. The gruesome nature of the crimes, the precision with which they were carried out, and the fact that the killer was never caught or identified make this case an enduring enigma.

A Glimpse into the Criminal Mind

As someone deeply interested in criminal psychology this experience allowed me to analyse the Ripper's actions. It's chilling to think about the level of sadism and psychopathy that may have driven this killer.

The Jack the Ripper Walk offers valuable insights into the mind of a serial killer, helping us understand the many dark corners of human behaviour.

Conclusion

The Jack the Ripper walk in London is not merely a historical tour; it's a chilling voyage into the depths of criminal psychology. It opened my eyes to the character and behaviour of this notorious serial killer, leaving me with a profound sense of fascination and unease. The mystery of Jack the Ripper ensures a testament to the enduring allure of true crime and the human capacity for darkness.

If you have an opportunity to visit London, I highly recommend taking this unforgettable journey through the streets of Whitechapel. It may just leave you with a deeper understanding of the haunting criminal mindset of Jack the Ripper.

Part 10
Close

I have chosen to finish this book with Jack the Ripper, as for many this is where the fascination with serial killers started and has grown ever since, there were earlier killers, but none that have captivated audiences worldwide for so long.

We all know the outcome, but still every new remake still has millions of viewers. As humans our innate curiosity for the macabre and the speculation of what if, holds as firm today as it did centuries ago.

There are many stories of perpetrators and these that I have included is not to enhance or highlight them, but to raise awareness mainly of their plausibility, which helps each and every one of them find a way to entice another victim, awareness, understanding and knowledge will make a difference for individuals, plus all the amazing technical and scientific detection aids of today's law enforcement helps to detect and capture violent perpetrators faster than before.

Thank you for joining me in this compilation of writings, I hope you have found some insights and maybe even some lightbulb moments in these pages.

ABOUT THE AUTHOR

Linda Sage is originally from Kent and return regularly to see family and friends, but now she lives in her lovely, adopted city of Leeds.

As a young person, she had never been involved with crime, police or the justice system, but she has always been fascinated by the darkest facets of human behaviour. The choices she chose caused quite a stir. Many of her friends were curious and inquisitive, which has only increased over the years, but her father was devastated. He wanted her to be a doctor or lawyer and saw no value in her chosen interest.

Linda learned very early that she needed an outlet to distract her from work and completely focus on something else. For Linda that's radio. She started out in hospital radio and local radios. She says, "It's a wonderful distraction as there's so much to think about, which means I have to be fully absorbed. It's also an opportunity to share my favourite music and meet wonderful people from all walks of life."

Linda's other favourite thing to do is to travel, and one of her recent trips was a winter cruise to Norway where she rode a husky sledge and snowmobile in -30 degree temperatures.

She is committed to educating and informing

others about the motivations driving society's most heinous criminals. She is equally passionate about educating the public to recognise early warning signs, as well as ways they can remove themselves from dangerous situations such as coercive control and domestic violence.

Although she is now retired from the day-to-day rigor of working in prisons, she still enjoys writing and sharing her insights and knowledge.

True Crime People & Places

True Crime People & Places

True Crime People & Places